The Last Traces
of *Hope*

A Novel

By

N. Madera Aguilar

Print Edition: **CreateSpace**

To All Midshipmen

Contents

Prologue: **The Fear**........................... 9
Part 1: **The Inroad**
Chapter One 13
Chapter Two 21
Chapter Three 27
Part 2: **Raging Moments**
Chapter Four 39
Chapter Five 45
Chapter Six 56
Chapter Seven 72
Part 3: **Loss of Hope**
Chapter Eight 85
Chapter Nine 95
Chapter Ten 103
Chapter Eleven 112
Chapter Twelve 120
Chapter Thirteen 127
Part 4: **Turnovers**
Chapter Fourteen 137
Chapter Fifteen 145
Chapter Sixteen 154
Chapter Seventeen 163
Chapter Eighteen 173
Chapter Nineteen 183
Chapter Twenty 190
Part 5: **As Fate Would Have It**
Chapter Twenty-one 201
Epilogue: **And Hope, too**.... 211

Prologue

Prologue: The Fear

The unsettling events that transpired during the last few days of July, 1990 exacerbated the volatile situation in the Mideast, particularly Kuwait, and it sent Brian Rios, the Deputy Employment and Welfare Attaché assigned in that small nation, worrying. He was working on a report to be submitted to the Middle East Coordinator's Office in Manila but the vexation in his mind had affected his writing. He simply could not finish the paper work.

The relations between Kuwait and its neighbor, Iraq, had deteriorated and this drove Brian into fear. Any further worsening of such relations could place him in a precarious situation. As the Kuwait-based DEWA of his country, he was watching over thousands of Filipinos working in that country alone—tens of thousands, in fact. He was next in rank to the Employment and Welfare Attaché who was based in Riyadh, Saudi Arabia, and in charge of providing for and overseeing the employment and welfare needs of all the overseas contract workers in the Mideast. The latter carried the appellation of EWA. Naturally, Brian was always referred to as the DEWA by his countrymen in Kuwait.

The dispute between Iraq and Kuwait had been escalating day after day. The most recent developments pouring in from both countries did not augur well for peace. Brian saw to it that he was kept fully abreast of news updates from the two countries.

A bulletin furnished him by diplomatic sources read in part: "... *even the Organization of Islamic Conference, made up of forty-eight members had urged the two fellow member-states to resort to peaceful means in resolving their differences. Iraqi President Saddam Hussein, however, is hard on his demands that Kuwait cut oil production, pay for oil allegedly pumped from the border which Iraq claims as part of its territory and write off billions of dollars in loan.*"

And as he further leafed through the pages, Brian arrived at the concluding statement: "... *on the part of Kuwait, its demands focus on the withdrawal of Iraq's forces from the 160-kilometer border. It views such massing of Iraqi forces as a threat. The withdrawal is a pre-condition to the holding of any negotiation. This, apparently, is Kuwait's position.*"

Brian could no longer conceal the fact that he was on the verge of panic. He feared that the consequences would be beyond estimation should the talks between the two countries fail.

Part 1:
The Inroad

Chapter One

It was the twenty-fourth of July, 1990 and Captain Porfirio Villar had just turned fifty. Already, he was beginning to entertain the idea that since lately he had gone down to being some sort of a Midas in reverse: everything he touched seemed to turn into stone. He decided, anyhow, to proceed with the celebration and the bridge, this time, had become a rowdy place—in contrast to what it was supposed to be and had always been: the hallmark of quietude. It was here that precision was being guarded to the fullest. *And it was here too that mistakes were committed, the effect of which was still taking its toll on him. For one, he permitted his men to do welding jobs at the port side of the ship while they were on the high seas, which he should not have done so. For another, he allowed his men to do battle with pirates in Western Africa, resulting in the death of one of the marauders when they could simply have left them behind as the latter had slower boat. One good thing though was that nobody got hurt among the crew members.* But then, today was an extraordinary moment.

"You can go on but the officers on watch should always be on the alert and may join in only after relief," he instructed as he prepared to leave the bridge.

"Aye, aye, sir!" some of them chorused.

"Hail to the master!" someone from the group voiced out.

"Hail!" all of them echoed, followed by the raising of the hands with glasses and squeaking sounds as if there were breakages.

"I'll be in my cabin."

"Good night, captain," Alan Blancaflor, the apprentice mate bade.

"And happy birthday, sir!" almost all of them shouted.

***

Some nautical miles away, a naval vessel was roaming the vast and almost boundless Arabian Sea. Dean S. Eaglewood, a navy ensign on board, was taking things lightly while another man, apparently his subordinate, was busy with his hands on certain gadgets and his eyes on what appeared to be a modern screen wide enough to be mistaken for a home entertainment tube.

"What's the latest, Brundy?" Ensign Eaglewood asked.

"It appears that this thing is headed for Kuwait," Brundy responded.

"Well, that's interesting. Tag it."

"I think we should, sir. I'll be doing it."

***

Inside his cabin, Captain Villar prepared to take a respite from the grueling day. The job in the bridge had to be done and an assurance that the ship should always be fit had likewise to be upheld. Yet, this day, a celebration could not be denied his men as they had already been wont to it for the past couple of years. He was glad though that it was almost over as the night deepened.

As he was lying down and beginning to close his eyes, the reminiscence of the past suddenly came to him. The graduation scene at the maritime academy in the Philippines' capital city, Manila, once again unfolded in his mind and the vivid portrayal of his role as his class' top ranking cadet, which he had always cherished, re-emerged.

The same scene unfurled as the apprentice mate Alan engaged in reverie after the celebration attained its finale and time came for him to go into respite in his quarters. After the mess had been fixed by him and the ordinary seaman, there was nothing to busy himself with for the rest of the nocturnal stretch, thus, other thoughts had to be entertained before sleep finally set in. The setting, however, differed as the number of years in between was simply too large. In his imagination, the graduation rites were carried out quite pompously, with him taking an outstanding role as, just like Villar, he finished the course as the most outstanding graduate. He was topnotcher of Class '89, a feat Villar achieved in the '60s. Both of them belonged to the same Alma Mater, one reason perhaps, aside from his potentials, why it did not take him so hard to get into Villar's ship.

In Villar's mind, the ceremonies commenced as midshipmen—maritime cadets—in their white gala uniform marched toward the front of a stage where graduation rites were to be conducted. Flashes of the cameras produced a momentary blinding effect on him as his turn to take his slot came. The ensuing program was highlighted by an announcement that he made it on top of the class. Praises heaped upon him seemed endless.

In Alan's recollection, the march the band played as he went up the stage to be pinned with tokens of achievement by his father and mother overwhelmed his emotion. He embraced both of them with a profuse outpouring of gratitude after a medal and a ribbon became visible on his breast.

A raucous restaurant scene, where food was sumptuous and drinks flowed, followed the graduation events which featured topnotcher Villar.

It was a different scene which came after Alan's own. A graduation ball was held for the graduates in one of Manila's gleaming hotels and this was attended by Alan with his girlfriend Tina. Males were in their coat-and-tie best while females wore gowns. Most of their companions were dancing merrily but Alan and Tina were engaged in serious conversation.

"Are you leaving me soon, Alan?" Tina asked.

"Tina, we've come to a point in our lives where we have to walk the path that is destined for us," Alan answered.

"Why did you have to choose this kind of occupation?"

"I simply found that this is the right one for me. I will be leaving but it's only temporary. I'll keep coming back, you'll see."

Alan and Tina walked out of the ballroom, crossed the hotel lobby and proceeded to an area beside a swimming pool. They sat together and held each other's hands.

"Hey, Alan, not having a slot upstairs? Hurry and get one. This night's the queen of all nights," a passing guy taunted Alan upon seeing him with Tina. He and his girl were up to something.

"Of course, it is. There'll be princes and princesses soon," Alan responded.

Tina poked a finger at Alan's waist, a reminder that there was no necessity for his statement. But the two men just laughed.

"Baby, your guy's a good one. He'll handle you well. Good luck," Alan's friend, after leaning to take a good look at Tina, took his girlfriend's arm and led her away from them.

"Who was that?" she asked Alan.

"A classmate, Dennis Nillos. Graduated, too. The girl with him is his new one ... after the break-up with the first."

Later, they approached the front desk and negotiated for a room. When they entered the one assigned to them, Alan began touching the switches and left only a single flickering bulb. He and Tina soon opted to make love.

***

Their recounts over and both of them now slumbering, the captain and his apprentice mate had no inkling as to what was going on in a different ship quite far from them sailing on another portion of the sea, but the occupants of which maintained a steady, watchful eye on their vessel.

"Ho-humn …"

Brundy kept hearing this from his immediate superior until he found that it was the last one from him. But he did not turn to look at the latter since his eyes were captured by the screen he was faced with.

"They have somehow reduced speed. Ah … they'll be docking in Kuwait. It's quite certain …" Brundy intoned while still being engrossed with the object on the screen.

No reaction having been received from Eaglewood, Brundy turned his head and saw that the ensign was immobile with his eyes shut. And the latter started snoring.

* * *

The Qasrah Regal Hotel stood as an imposing four-storey edifice inside a fenced complex, with all the facilities surrounding it, situated at the southernmost outlying district of Kuwait City. It had a well-landscaped setting, adequately sized pool and wide parking space. It was the city's newest tourist attraction and a haven for foreigners although it was smaller than the famed multi-national five-star lodgments. Yet, it was just as luxurious and even more accommodating. Its staff was trained to be clientele-oriented and the motto *'the guest is always right'* was adhered upon by all employees, most of whom were citizens of different Asian countries. Even though the staffers were of diverse nationalities, each one had his own contribution to make it the guest's perception that the *QRH* provided the feeling of being at home away from home.

The hotel had been fully booked during the first half of July, 1990 but when the third week came there was a marked reduction of reservations with statistics going steadily downward. On the last week of the month, less than half the total number of rooms were occupied. On the first day of August, 1990, more guests had checked out.

"Your beau is checking out too, Myra?" a uniformed girl at the reception counter asked a similarly attired employee beside her. The former was checking things out and appeared ready to leave.

"He will, tomorrow. His liberty has expired and his ship is leaving the day after, Tanya," Myra replied.

"Can you tell me how this seaman landed into your lap, Myra?"

"I was the one who landed on his, Tanya."

And they both laughed.

"By the way, more guests are leaving. Did you notice that, Myra?"

"Yes, how come…?"

"I think they're being unnerved by the news of word war between Kuwait and Iraq.

Myra was intrigued by Tanya's statement. But it was cut short by the sight of his boyfriend coming.

"There he is approaching us," Myra said, lifting her bag. "Thanks so much for being accommodating to him, I mean, for lending your space in our room to him, Tanya."

"Ah, don't mention it. It's a matter of one day. Besides, I'm on night duty and we have the available quarters in the hotel," Tanya responded as Myra edged herself out of the counter to join her boyfriend.

"Hi," the latter waved to Tanya.

"Hi … Go on and enjoy…." And Tanya smiled meaningfully.

Chapter Two

The vessel with stripes of blue, yellow and red on its funnel was docked at the international port of Kuwait City. After several days of unloading its cargo intended for the port city, it was all set to sail on August 2, 1990 although the ETD posted on a billboard at the pier stated *1800 HRS, 03 Aug 1990*. It was merely waiting for its chandler who seemed to have incurred delay and Captain Porfirio Villar thought that the allowance for his boat's estimated time of departure was but appropriate. He had prepared this ship for a voyage that would take him and his men to another destination.

He was standing in the bridge with a telescope hanging from his neck when he heard distant sounds of explosion. He gazed at a distance, looking at a black smoke rising towards the sky. Although bothered, he believed it would not affect them since they were on board a commercial vessel of foreign registry.

Alan entered the bridge wearing a chambray apprentice mate's uniform. He was holding a cup and saucer with steaming black coffee which he immediately handed to the master. The latter, without hesitation, sipped at the cup and savored the brew.

More sounds of explosion resonated and the captain observed dark billows of smoke appearing at the skyline which seemed to multiply.

"Is there war going on here? I wonder what this is," Villar uttered.

Alan was speechless. He simply stared at the captain with looks of perplexity.

"Tell all of the officers to come to the bridge," the master ordered Alan.

"The chief officer's sick, sir. He has fever. The third mate is coming after me," Alan replied.

"The second officer?"

"He's on liberty, sir."

"He was, four days ago. Both of you left this ship on pass in the morning of that day. While you returned in the afternoon, he stayed on shore. Does that last to this day? His leave expired yesterday," the captain stressed.

"He hasn't returned since he disembarked on the first day of his leave, sir," Alan told Villar. "We went to the Qasrah Regal Hotel together. His girlfriend works there as an overseas contract worker, a co-employee of my fiancee's sister, Tanya, who's a year older than my girl, Tina. We both visited them. He checked in at the hotel as I left."

"I have been expecting him to report today. For the time being, the third mate will take over his job. You will assume the latter's functions," the captain said.

"Sir?" Alan exhibited surprise, but it was coupled with unexpected glee.

"You're learning fast, Alan. After a year of apprenticeship, you appear ready to take on the officer's job. It's a matter of time and you'll be issued a license," the master commented.

Alan took pleasure on what he considered an accolade from his superior when the third mate entered the bridge.

"Sir, there are soldiers poised to board the ship," the vessel's third mate informed Captain Villar after entering the bridge. He was earlier summoned by the captain for a different task.

"Soldiers?"

"Yes, sir, soldiers," the third mate stressed.

The ship's master was perplexed. He immediately dispensed with the cup of coffee, walked out of the bridge and went straight to the starboard side of the vessel which faced the pier.

The soldiers were already at the other end of the gangplank when he saw them. They were about twenty, and when their commander saw the ship captain, the former walked through the gangplank to board the ship—followed by his men. Obviously, they were not Kuwaitis.

"Who's in command of this vessel?" the soldiers' commander asked.

"I'm the master of this ship," Captain Villar told him.

No handshake transpired between the two officers.

"I'm Major Abu Qassif. I have instructions from Baghdad," the Iraqi officer told the ship captain.

"May we know what they are, and why?" the master asked.

"Iraq has absorbed Kuwait into its territories. This ship will have to remain in Kuwait City until further orders," Major Qassif announced.

"No, that's piracy!" the captain protested.

"Call it what you will, but we are doing this in the name of the noble cause which our country upholds for the good of the entire Middle East. We have reclaimed Kuwait for integration to our dear Iraq," the major spoke sternly, sidetracking the captain's indignation.

Captain Villar wanted to say something more to Major Qassif but the latter immediately turned his back on him and motioned his hands with instructions for his soldiers to leave.

After two steps on the gangplank, he turned his head and spoke to Captain Villar: "I'll be back tomorrow for more instructions. I have so many things to attend to today. Just stay put as guards will oversee the pier and keep watch on your vessel."

Long after the Iraqi major had left, Captain Villar remained dumbfounded and was shaken in disbelief. His men who had gathered around him were speechless, unsure of how to react to what had just transpired. Their faces epitomized the confusion that suddenly engulfed their being while fear began to build in them.

"Tell everybody to come to the mess hall for a meeting," the captain announced. Although it was primarily directed at the apprentice mate, Alan was sure he had lesser job to do as almost everybody on the deck was present. He needed merely to contact the engine people.

"Aye, aye, sir!" and Alan quickly left.

When he showed up later at the start of the meeting, he had news to bring—the chief mate's condition seemed to have worsened as his body temperature kept on rising.

"Just stay with him all the time, Alan, and make sure that his medication is precisely attended to. This time you'll be doing the second mate's job," the captain instructed Alan.

This caused a light moment to prevail in the meeting as some subdued smiles flashed on the faces of those present. The second mate acted as the ship's doctor.

"You'll be doing the second mate's job even before you assume the third mate's functions, Alan," the ship's quartermaster commented. The smiles sported by some of them turned into chuckles. The QM was perhaps the captain's most trusted personally on the deck.

As Alan left the hall, Ben Gomez, the third mate, arrived. He was the last one to join the meeting and had some information to share with those present.

"He told me he was seeing a girlfriend employed at the Qasrah Regal Hotel which is Kuwait City's farthest from here. I think he stayed there for the duration of his liberty," the third mate averred, referring to the second mate.

"Well, I think Peter can manage. He does well in judo and karate being a red-belter. He can ward off a trouble maker whom he may encounter. Besides, his Indian profile could have him mistaken as an Iraqi,"

Arthur Ng, the ship's quartermaster interjected. Nobody, however, took him seriously.

"The situation's getting more complicated for us," the captain was shaking his head as he spoke. "First, there's war. It merely waited for us here. Now, we got stuck to it. Suddenly, each one of us seems to be falling into its snare."

As they listened to the ship master's speech, the faces of those present had turned sullen. They were beginning to realize that, with them trapped in the arena of conflict, the captain had shuddered at the thought of future events.

Chapter Three

Just before daybreak on August 3, 1990, a military van was cruising along one of the streets in the outskirts of Kuwait City carrying six uniformed Iraqi soldiers. It was driven by a sergeant and seated beside him was a lieutenant. Two privates were behind them while the remaining two were positioned further back. It was negotiating the road slowly when the lieutenant ordered the driver to stop.

The lieutenant disembarked and the rest of the soldiers followed him. He stood in front of a five-unit apartment and found that one of the units, particularly the middle of the five, had its light on in the ground level. The leader walked to the door and signaled his soldiers to break it open. Two of the privates obliged. They raised their rifles and alternately hit the knob with the butts of their long arms until the door gave way.

The Iraqi officer, finding nobody in the ground level of the apartment unit, removed his pistol from its holster with his right hand while his left made a sign for the four privates to remain as he and the sergeant were to ascend the stairway leading to the second level.

In one of the three rooms upstairs, a couple cringed, apparently having been roused by the noise caused by the breaking of the door downstairs. The door of the room, meanwhile, swung open after having been banged and the Iraqi lieutenant, followed by the sergeant, appeared. They looked at each other and the sergeant stepped back, closing the door of the room upon exit and went downstairs to join the privates while grinning.

The lieutenant stepped toward the couple, pointing his pistol at the man's chest while the woman screamed.

"Nooo!"

The man suddenly lunged at the lieutenant, grabbing his hand holding the pistol which went off. They wrestled for the position of the handgun which fired again, hitting the Iraqi on his stomach. The woman continued screaming while the man threw karate chops on the lieutenant to finish him off. The lieutenant dropped on the floor.

"Hurry, let's take the fire escape stairs through the window," the man ordered the woman, grabbing his companion's outer garment hung on the wall and throwing it to the woman who was only in her nightwear. The man was wearing shorts and a sleeveless shirt with print: *Second Mate, M/V Hope.* They descended from the room through its window as fast as they could using the fire escape stairs made of steel.

Meanwhile, on the first floor of the apartment unit, the Iraqi sergeant could not stop grinning as he faced the four privates who too wore smiles in their faces.

"Vintage style of the lieutenant," said the sergeant. "Loves to take a girl with a mate. Enjoying while she screams and finishing lover with two shots. Wants it very private, though."

Moments dragged on and the smiles on the soldiers' faces gradually disappeared. The sergeant's turned sour.

"He doesn't do it that long. I know he's a quick reliever. Why is he still there?"

His companions could not answer him.

Several minutes more passed and the sergeant could not take it anymore. He ambled through the steps of the stairway and leaned on the door of the room.

"Sir?"

Getting no answer, the sergeant decided to open the door himself. What he saw shocked him. The lieutenant was lying on the bloodied floor, seemingly lifeless. The man and the woman were nowhere to be found.

"Hurry up! Get quick! Let's take him to the hospital," the sergeant turned frantic. His companions found it difficult to prioritize their moves.

***

Ship Captain Porfirio Villar had long been wide awake and, as a matter of fact, was on the verge of finishing his first cup of coffee for the day when daylight descended. He gazed at the smoldering skyline and observed that the bombardment at dawn of this day was heavier than that of the previous day. To him, this became a hint that the events of the preceding day were here to stay. He could not fathom the depth of Qassif's designs, especially on how long they were holding his ship from sailing. And why they were doing so, he had not the faintest idea.

The unexpected disappearance of his second officer had remained a puzzle to Captain Villar since the day Peter Singh was supposed to return to his ship. Now, as he had emptied his cup while standing in the flying bridge and staring at the recycled hue of the sky, his presumption that something untoward might have happened to his Indian *mestizo* second officer became more concrete. His doubts could be as true as the crimson sky now being unraveled before his eyes.

The second day of the occupation of Kuwait—and for that matter of his vessel—by the Iraqi forces was now fully unfurled as sunburst had its fallout all over the area. The master's attempt at getting a cue on why they were being held indefinitely in the port of Kuwait proved futile. It was a burden trying to solve the puzzle of why they had to remain moored indefinitely. They could be sailing to move out of the Gulf area now had they not been held at port for unknown reasons.

"I need another cup, Alan," the captain told the apprentice mate. He was a heavy coffee drinker.

"I'll bring you another cup, sir," Alan obliged. He had proven himself to be attentive to the needs of his superiors and this made the captain conclude that he would make a good officer someday.

When Alan came back, he handed to the master a steaming cup of the latter's brew prepared according to his specifications. Villar wanted it black with low sugar. Alan was glad that it would take hours before the master would again require him to get ready with the specified brew. It was only the distance from the first to the second cup which seemed too brief.

"How's Eldon?" Villar asked after his first sip of the second cup. He was referring to Eldon Ramos, the chief mate.

"His temperature has stabilized, sir, and it seems he is in better situation now than yesterday."

The captain just nodded. Then he asked Alan: "Ready for the chores of third mate?"

"Quite ready, sir," Alan smilingly answered.

"Good."

As he sipped some more at his cup, Villar laid down a plan.

"Tell the third officer to have coffee with me," the captain ordered the apprentice mate.

In a few minutes, the third mate joined them in the bridge.

"You'll be acting second officer," Captain Villar announced to his third officer.

"Sir?" the latter did not expect it.

"Yes, you will."

"And..."

"You begin transferring some of the third mate's responsibilities to Alan. He can tackle the job. He'll be acting third officer. It's a matter of time and he'll be issued a license."

Alan was elated. He was the last to expect what he had just heard.

"And Peter, sir?" the third mate managed to complete what he wanted to utter.

"I don't think Peter is going to ever show up," the captain said, emptying his second cup of coffee.

Alan received the utensils, consisting of cup and saucer, from the master and placed them on a tray for disposal. As he was getting the petty things done, he reminisced the early days he spent on board the *M/V Hope*, learning to do tasks the way the captain wanted them done. He was quick to receive his instructions and was ready to adapt to his lifestyle on board. The captain was a man who had penchant for details and was very particular about order and precision on board.

Outstanding as a midshipman and a fast learner on the deck, Alan believed he had all the readiness to become a third mate.

***

Despite their being already seated, albeit uncomfortably, beside a pool at the Qasrah Regal Hotel, one of Kuwait's highly rated, the couple could still hardly catch up with breath.

"Don't worry, Myra, we'll get through with this," the man said, calming down his tense girlfriend.

"Why did you have to do it, Peter?" Myra asked her lover, rubbing her eyes with her fingers to quell the tears which were beginning to form again.

"What else would I have done? It's instinct. My training in an advanced reserved naval course would have been useless if I did not apply the basics of what I learned. Besides, it's a matter of self-preservation."

"What if they would hunt us?

"You should be glad we're in this hotel. At least we're safe for the time being," Peter said, trying to seek reassurance.

"It wasn't easy getting in here. I never experienced in my whole life leaving a two-storey house through a window, inching my way through narrow passages under the cover of a fleeting darkness, dressed unusually..." Myra stressed.

"I was attired like being in an early morning jog," Peter tried to be funny but Myra was solemn.

"Not me. I was a puzzling woman when I entered the hotel premises. The way I was dressed, that is. Good thing the guard knows me. Not a lot of people are around ... Thank God, there was no untoward ... It wasn't easy, really ..."

There was silence for a while.

"The guests were frantically leaving yesterday, some saying they'd shun the invasion. The hotel's almost empty now. And then, such thing which just happened to us. What's behind this occurrence, Pete?" Myra sought for an answer.

"My fears have materialized, Myra. The Iraqis are here," Peter answered.

***

As the sun moved up higher in the sky, the exploding sounds were getting fewer. The heat which subsumed the coolness of dawn had become unrelenting as Villar waited for Qassif to return but it appeared that there was still no shadow of him although it was nearing high noon.

After taking his lunch, the captain went to the gangplank but found no sign of Qassif's arrival.

Instead, his eyes got irritated by the unsightly moves of Qassif's guards in the vicinity of the gangplank's entry point along the pier. They held their weapons as if they were ready to fire in an instant and looking up at the ship like a hunter seeking for a target.

When the captain was convinced that Qassif was not coming back at all, he decided to take a nap. He was about to depart from his fleeting consciousness when a commotion took place on board the vessel. This brought him to total wakefulness and a finding that Qassif had arrived. The latter had more men with him this time.

***

Myra had finished packing up her belongings at the hotel. It was nearly noontime. She had requested for a three-day leave of absence from the hotel management and was subsequently allowed such avail, given the circumstances prevailing.

Myra went to the hotel's locker room and emptied her locker with contents of personal effects. She was glad that her credit card was left there as she would make use of the same in paying the hotel's *Items Shoppe* for new sets of apparel she and Peter purchased to have something new to change with. After having placed all the articles from her locker in a large-sized shoulder bag, Myra passed by the reception counter and intended to exchange parting words with three other employees, two males and a female, who were in the midst of a conversation.

"Are you really a Sri Lankan, Derik?" the Filipina receptionist was questioning one of her male companions.

"Actually, my mother's a Filipina and my father a Sri Lankan. I carry the citizenship of my father, Tanya. And that's why friends and acquaintances have always referred to me as the Sri Lankan," Derik explained.

"I see … unlike Elmo here, a full-bloodied Manilenio," Tanya said.

"Of course," Elmo confirmed.

"Excuse me, but I'll be off now," Myra found an occasion to butt in.

"Take care," they said to Myra.

"Thanks. Take care, too, the three of you. Elmo, Derik, be on guard for Tanya," she uttered as she waved goodbye to them. Tanya was assigned at the reception counter, Derik a valet and Elmo a driver of the hotel.

"We'll miss you Myra," Derik intoned as Myra was moving away.

"You're not hiding the tone of despair in your voice, Derik," Tanya commented with Myra getting more distant. Meanwhile, Elmo just flashed a meaningful smile on his face.

"How can I…?"

"Brush it off, Derik. Your crush on Myra will only bring you more sadness as you continue to cherish it. She's so attached to him now," Tanya counseled the valet.

Myra left the hotel in the company of Peter who carried her shoulder bag through the side gate. After standing at the road side for a few minutes, an empty taxi was chanced upon by them as it made a right turn from the nearest road junction. They immediately boarded the vehicle when it stopped beside them.

"Get fast please, we're in a hurry," Myra requested the driver.

Their destination was the Philippine Embassy in Kuwait City.

As the cab swiftly negotiated the road and turned left at the next junction, a column of military vehicles with a tank at the tail end arrived at the hotel.

Part 2:
Raging Moments

Chapter Four

Captain Villar quickly moved and hied himself to the gangplank but Qassif was already on the deck when he met him. Without hesitation, the Iraqi major made an announcement.

"We are replacing the complement of this ship with our own people. Only the captain and his chief officer are to remain on board. The rest will have to disembark as our own personnel will now take over," Major Qassif made clear his instructions.

"No! Over my dead body!" the captain's voice boomed, his blood pressure rising and at the same time maintaining a steadfast posture. He would have thrown a mailed fist at the major's mouth had it not been for the fact that dozens of guns were supporting the Iraqi officer's back.

"In that case, dead bodies will be floating overboard," the Iraqi officer coldly remarked.

"Captain, please…. Major, give us a moment," Chief Mate Ramos, who had just arrived aided by Third Mate Gomez, interceded, pacifying their superior officer and shoving him away from the Iraqi as they whispered something to him.

"Sir, we are in no bargaining position. They have staged an invasion. They are waging war," the chief mate intoned, appearing to have prevailed upon the former to calm down as they retreated several steps from the major.

As the chief and third officers pleaded with Villar, the tense situation was diffused. Qassif merely looked at them nonchalantly while maintaining an alert, hard and fast stance.

"A moment, major ..." Chief Officer Ramos addressed Qassif with his right hand raised as if seeking permission to do something.

The major, saying nothing, just stared sternly at the three seamen as they stepped back farther and withdrew toward the bridge at the upper deck as the tension ebbed completely.

Meanwhile, Alan remained immobile, gazing in amazement at the major and his men. He saw, instead, that his world was crumbling down. Minutes earlier, he had built a dream so grand and beautiful. Now, he found it disintegrating into pieces.

Swayed by his subordinates' insistent pleading with him, Captain Villar's rage died down. He had finally come to a realization that it would be futile for him to maintain a combative posture. Sitting down and composing himself, he issued instructions to the chief mate.

"Tell that intruder I alone would like to remain in this ship if they have available personnel up to the level of chief officer and engineer," the captain ordered the chief mate.

"But, sir, the two of us are needed on board," Chief Mate Ramos protested.

"No. Leave this matter for me alone to deal with. I've been a ship master for the good part of my life.

The rest of you still have to work out a future for your selves. Go, find a way out of this if you can," the captain indicated he needed no further argument on his desire.

With motions of his hands, the master dismissed his chief officer and the latter reluctantly left the bridge, proceeding to where Major Qassif stood in order to make known Villar's desire.

Qassif at first tried to think it over.

Then he said: "Our complement will be arriving from Baghdad this afternoon. I think we can dispense with everybody, including mates and engineers, as we have enough technical men and volunteers to run this vessel. We only need the captain as our link to the owners of this ship and as communicator on our behalf."

"I'll relay the information to the captain," and Ramos slowly moved, returning to the bridge.

Arriving there, he apprised the captain of the Iraqi's response.

"He's amenable to your wishes, sir."

"Good. Don't waste time then. Have all your belongings ready for disembarkation. The men, too, instruct them."

"It pains me to leave you alone here, sir," the chief mate intoned, exhibiting an air of sadness.

"It would be more painful if you stay behind," the master coldly remarked. He would have intended to assuage his sailing mate's heavy emotions but did not produce the desired results as Ramos sobbed.

It was then that Alan entered the bridge followed by Third Mate Gomez.

The two highest officers of the ship were prompted to turn their heads.

"Sir, what recourse do we have now?" Alan asked, his face sporting an expression of bewilderment. His grim mood was shared by the third mate.

Villar skirted his apprentice mate's question and went direct to the point. He said: "Alan, I was building a grand dream for you. But circumstances have reduced everything to pieces. I wanted to touch you a gold, but it seems that a stone is what I instead produced. You should hurry, pack your things up and leave the ship. Nothing is certain now."

"Sir ..." Third Mate Gomez wanted to say something too but he was at a loss for words.

The captain turned to him. "You, too, Ben ... Lose no time in leaving. This is my ship. I go where they take it."

Gomez showed an expression of despair in his face. His pained looks exacerbated the prevailing mood in the bridge.

Less than an hour later, a squad of sailors was seen flowing down the gangplank of *M/V Hope*. Each seaman was carrying his own packs and belongings. Tailing the line was a disappointed Alan and he carried the heaviest of faces. Immediately before him was the chief mate who was so saddened by what they got into. The quartermaster headed the line followed by the third mate. The engineers and other members of the complement were in between.

Captain Villar stood on the ship's side alley, his hands holding the railing. For the last time, he and Alan looked at each other before the latter finally went down the gangplank. The captain flashed an uneasy smile and a thumbs-up sign. He likewise acknowledged the last glance from his chief officer with a nod. When he turned around he found Qassif with his back on the railing but watching him through a side glance. As he passed by him, the major uttered words as if whispering.

"Tomorrow the ship will start loading its cargoes," the Iraqi said.

Villar just looked at Qassif but did not say a word. He went direct to the bridge.

Meanwhile, the group of dislodged seamen from the ship *M/V Hope* who were already on the wharf found that there was a yellow commuter service bus waiting for them in one of the port's perimeter limits. Dusk was already setting in and it was getting hazy fast. The sailors walked toward the vehicle in single file guided by four Iraqi troopers who led them to the bus.

When not one of the four soldiers was looking at him as he was at the end of the file, Alan suddenly detached himself from the group unnoticed and hid between a pile of cargoes they had passed by. He further inched himself through the narrow alley created by the space between the heap of loads and slowly crawled deep into the inner storage area inside the port limits. When Chief Mate Ramos turned his head before boarding the bus, he was shocked to find Alan was no longer behind him. But he kept it to himself. The guards perhaps failed to notice or they didn't care at all. It was getting dark and they were not particular about their captives' number.

When all of the seamen had embarked on the bus, the vehicle left the harbor with four Iraqi guards on board. Alan, who remained unnoticed, peeped through a space between two crates from a distance and saw the departing bus until it vanished from his sight.

"Where are we bound for?" Third Mate Gomez who was seated behind the driver asked the latter.

"They're taking you to Baghdad," the driver answered without looking at the third officer.

Seated behind the third mate was the chief officer who heard the conversation but did not seem to care as his mind lingered. He was sure Alan had not gotten into the bus and still, instinct prompted him to look around. It was a confirmation that the apprentice mate had gone elsewhere. The Iraqis nevertheless remained unconcerned as they ordered the bus driver to proceed to their destination. Either they missed what was supposed to be the total number of passengers escorted by them or they did not care at all if such total was minus one. As the bus was speeding toward the desert, gloom commenced to descend.

Chapter Five

Earlier in the afternoon of August 3, 1990, when Peter and Myra arrived at the Philippine Embassy in Kuwait, they immediately looked for the Deputy Employment and Welfare Attache but he was not in his office. His secretary told them that Brian Rios, the DEWA, was busy somewhere in the embassy premises attending to the multitude of Filipinos who had sought refuge therein, mostly runaways from their employers.

At the Philippine Embassy in the Kuwaiti capital, a throng of people seeking refuge was simply an awesome sight. The explosions they heard at first signs of the inroad on Kuwait had jolted them and sent chills to their nerves, prompting some to flee their residences without ado and others to abandon their places of work. The eventual spread of uniformed Iraqis in the streets of Kuwait City drove them away, fleeing to the embassy compound. They were Filipinos, jobseekers who finally landed various kinds of employment in the Middle East, particularly in Kuwait. They grasped all sorts of employment contracts just to have an alternative to the scarcity of jobs at home. They had left their country hoping that with the earnings they would get from a foreign land they could improve the living conditions of their families back home, and also their own while away on a work mission. The way the circumstances had evolved now could obliterate all that.

"I don't have to wait for him, Myra, you'll be safe here. I have to go back to my ship. It's supposed to sail this afternoon," the second mate said to Myra.

"Are you still leaving me, Pete? I thought you'd stay with me all the time now," Myra held the arms of her beau.

"I am a sailor, Myra, and I have not yet retired from navigating."

Myra embraced Peter and started to weep.

"When will it stop? I mean your having to leave again ... and again?" Myra asked Peter after regaining her composure.

"It will, in the near future. We'll be together once more ... and be with each other forever when all things get done and its appointed time comes," Peter replied.

"Is my necklace with you, Pete?"

"No...."

"It wasn't in my locker at the hotel."

"Don't worry I'll buy you another one when I reach the next port."

"The pendant contains my picture."

"Pose for a better one. We'll attach it to a dearer jewelry," Peter whispered to Myra. He kissed her and left the embassy.

***

When the soldiers arrived at the Qasrah Regal Hotel after the departure of Peter and Myra earlier, reactions of those still there were varied: stunned silence, disturbance, panic and hysteria. The remaining few guests who were jolted from their shares of the *siesta* ran to the doors of their rooms and heads popped out almost simultaneously. Some chorused *'what's that'* in unison. One man nearly jumped out of the window until he realized that he was on the fourth floor of the hotel.

The appearance of the soldiers who started to pour in at the hotel caused the atmosphere of conviviality, which usually permeated the lobby, to be subsumed by a surging cloud of perplexed anxiety. There was certainty in the thinking of some occupants that the hotel could have been among the few establishments lately intruded to by the soldiers since they signaled their coming with explosions the day before. It was the farthest from the central portion of the downtown area, being situated in the southernmost outskirts of the city. The Iraqis came from the north. They realized that had they been so quick at all, they could have avoided the soldiers if they instantly left at the first bursts by cruising downwards to Saudi Arabia. But they had no inkling that the soldiers would reach their hotel. Those who had did not waste a single moment.

An uncanny fear struck the three employees of the hotel when one of the soldiers approached them. Tanya, the uniformed girl at the reception counter, was still conversing with Elmo and Derik when the uniformed man, a sergeant, asked her a question.

"This hotel is what they call *QRH*, right?"

"Yes, sir, the Qasrah Regal Hotel," Tanya answered.

Four other soldiers approached the sergeant. They were privates. One of them handed a necklace to him which the sergeant showed to Tanya.

"You know this girl, don't you?" he asked Tanya.

The hotel employee examined carefully the necklace presented to her by the sergeant, and to her consternation, it was Myra's picture in the pendant at the back of which the letters *QRH* were engraved. Her two male colleagues were aghast.

"You know her?" the sergeant repeated.

Tanya first cast a meaningful look at Elmo and Derik before answering the sergeant. "She must be a guest who already checked out."

"Why does she have a *QRH*?"

"Any guest can buy that at the *Items Shoppe*. Pardon me, sir, but why are you looking for her?" Tanya's reaction with an inquiry was spontaneous.

"She just killed our detachment commander!"

"Ugh!" Tanya coughed, as if she swallowed something hard. Her two male companions grimaced.

"That's incredible!" Elmo could no longer withhold comment.

"Why do you say so?" the sergeant turned his attention to him.

"I mean she's just a girl … as you said. How could she do it?"

The sergeant did not mind him anymore and instead turned to his four privates. "Let's go to the *Items Shoppe*."

***

Myra spent almost the entire afternoon waiting for the DEWA but he was simply being too busy with the other seekers of his attention. He was personally administering the registration and data-gathering of the persons who had sought shelter at the embassy. His office was grossly undermanned and its facilities could not provide the needed accommodation to be extended to the 'guests.' It would take time before she could get to him.

A long-haired woman about five years older than her approached Myra. "This situation is incredible," she said.

"You've been here since yesterday?" Myra asked her.

"Since early this morning, and I don't think we could get him to immediately whisk us out of here. He seems to be making all instructions to the welfare assistant. Isn't he planning to leave ahead of us?" the woman spoke anxiously.

"But why …"

The woman snapped Myra. "I have talked to two other women devising a more expedient plan. Listen to what they said."

And she whispered something to Myra.

***

It was being cast with darkness when the international port of Kuwait appeared in full view of Peter Singh. As he was approaching the gate of the port premises, he saw a yellow commuter service bus leaving the area. He crossed the road separating him from the gate and passed through the guard house. The sentry assigned at that particular hour was the one who had logged him out when he first left the pier and he instantly recognized him. The Iraqis had not relieved the guard.

"Didn't they take you too?" the sentry asked Peter.

"What do you mean?"

"It's your companions on that bus with the Iraqis."

"Whaat?" Peter could not believe what he had just heard. "I'll go to my ship anyway."

"Proceed, sir. The Iraqi soldiers may be waiting for you," said the guard.

"Huh?!" The puzzlement of Peter was total.

***

As the shadowy surroundings gripped him, Alan was at a loss on what to do and where to go. He had gone out of the port zone after inserting himself between crates and boxes, buildings and structures, fences and broken walls, sometimes almost crawling and at one instance climbing a six-foot high wire fence serving to mark the perimeter in order to completely extricate himself from the seafront tract of land.

He was too careful in not being seen by a couple or the few other individuals he happened to spot in a distance as he sought for a safer route in his unstoppable dash, deep into the city. Reducing himself into a mere silhouette whenever a trace of light or glimmer sometimes became inevitable while he was taking his route, Alan made sure that it was but momentary and could not draw attention.

Approaching the urban center, Alan noted that several deserted buildings were burned; he presumed that these were bombed by the Iraqis. He stopped beside a structure which was still smoldering and noted that it was a grocery store, burnt partially as there were items of merchandise still visible. He went inside slowly, careful not to injure or inflict pain upon himself, and found that there were food items he could still make use of. As these were canned or packed, he was certain the same could stave off his hunger. He started scavenging until his rummage paid off. There were even unscathed bottles of mineral water underneath the charred articles.

Alan located some partially damaged bags and culled those he could still make use of. He was able to lift two bags and strode to the back portion of a damaged edifice which turned out to be an abandoned storage compound. He positioned himself in what used to be a small warehouse and slouched over the used boxes. He lost no time in unpacking his spoils, consumed them and gulped the still warm contents of retrieved mineral water. His weariness sent him to slumber on top of the discarded cartons.

***

The bulbs atop the lampposts scattered along the extensive grounds of the harbor emitted bright lights and Peter immediately drew the attention of the soldiers guarding the *M/V Hope* and its berthing space when he arrived there.

One of the Iraqis accosted him, almost blocking his way.

"I'm the second officer of that ship," Peter told the trooper and, raising his arm, pointed his index finger to the vessel.

The confused soldier turned his head to the other guards who signaled him to lead Peter nearer the ship. When they reached the base of the gangplank, Major Qassif appeared before its upper end.

"What's the problem down there?"

"Sir, this man claims he is the second officer of that ship," one of the guards responded, almost shouting to ensure Qassif heard him.

"A second officer?" the major was stunned.

Calling his aide, he yelled: "Get the captain out here!"

A few minutes later, Captain Villar emerged and joined Qassif near the gangplank.

"Sir?" Peter called out upon being sure that it was Villar who showed up.

"Do you know that man?" Qassif asked the captain.

Villar was distraught but remained silent. He could not decipher what he was undergoing at that precise moment.

"I am asking you whether you know that guy who claims to be your second officer. Are you listening to me?" Qassif hollered at Villar.

"I don't know him," Villar coldly uttered.

"Get him out of here!" Qassif ordered his guards. "The captain says he doesn't know him. He's a fake, a nonsense."

"Captain Villar, it's me, Peter!" the second officer shouted. He was shocked at the unexpected turn of events. His voice had gone down to hoarseness as he cryingly blurted, "Are you out of your mind? What do you mean you don't know me? I am your second mate!"

As the captain and the major made themselves no longer available, the soldiers guarding the ship grabbed Peter by his arms and dragged him out of the port compound. He tried to ward them off and do battle with them but their sheer number made it impossible to let his chops and kicks triumph. In the end, he went down like a falling tree.

"You can't do this to me!" Peter continued to make known his protestations and misgivings at the top of his voice as the guards loaded him on a trailer and drove beyond the gate. The sentry who had earlier been accommodating to him could not believe what his eyes were seeing.

After being maneuvered out of the gate, the vehicle which carried the second mate stopped when it reached the nearest road junction. The soldiers instinctively pushed Peter off and drove back to the pier. The seaman agonized when his body went down flat on the road. As he screamed to let out the pains— in both body and spirit—a white-colored *Turtlehouse* crew cab passed by and sounded a loud 'screech' when it stopped beside him.

On board the *M/V Hope*, the Iraqi major went to the owner's cabin to retire. It was there where he billeted himself. Villar stayed at his captain's cabin, most of the time having his eyes shut while sulking in his bunk. When he opened them they were red.

***

When twilight came, it brought confusion to those who occupied the Philippine Embassy in Kuwait, and they lingered aimlessly, dawdling around without definite direction. Taking advantage of the crowd's uncertain mood, four women slipped by and surreptitiously left the embassy ground while nightfall was gradually taking over, running toward a waiting Kuwaiti police patrol car with two constables sitting in the front seat and expecting for them. The four women squeezed themselves at the back seat. The fourth passenger was Myra.

With all doors shut, the patrol car promptly pulled away from the scene.

"This is Corporal Charles Ubaud of the Kuwaiti Police, a special friend of Grace," the woman who earlier whispered something to Myra said. She pointed to a constable beside the driver and then turned to one of the domestic helpers who rode the car with them.

"Hello and thanks," Myra said.

"We'll take you to the pier and let you board a small boat bound for Basra," the corporal said. "A man will wait for you there and let you board a bus which will take you to Jordan. From there arrangements will be made to have you get back to your country."

"Oh, we're grateful. You're really so kind to us," Myra was profuse with thanks.

"I'm just returning a favor. Your friend Grace has done a lot, making me happy."

Myra moved her sight towards the domestic helper mentioned but Grace avoided seeing her eye-to-eye. The two other women seemed not to care.

"Pardon me, but you're Kuwaitis, right?" Myra asked, having turned to the constable once again.

"Of course. We just pretended as defectors to the Iraqis. Our car is flying their flag, you see? You're in safest hands."

When they were about to come nearer a junction that would lead them to the pier if they were to veer right, Myra saw a white-colored *Turtlehouse* crew cab parked beside the road while an obviously unconscious man was being loaded into the vehicle which instantaneously left the area even without having its doors fully shut yet.

The patrol car turned right at the junction and entered the port gate. The sentry at the guard house even rendered a salute. Myra saw that the pier was illuminated and soldiers abound. But they were all gathered near a large ship, not minding the small boats moored at the far end of the wharf.

Myra and her three companions disembarked from the patrol car and proceeded to one of the small boats. She noticed that Grace was the last one to get on board as she had to embrace the corporal and receive kisses from him. It did not take long and the boat left the pier.

Myra stared at the single large vessel which could be seen along the harbor. She was certain it was Peter's ship. She was thinking he could be well on board now returning to his chores.

Meanwhile, the white-colored *Turtlehouse* crew cab was speeding toward an unknown destination.

Chapter Six

As the soldiers loitered in the different parts of the hotel, the apprehensions of those seeing them intensified. Tanya was at the reception counter examining the contents of her handbag to make sure that everything she wanted it to contain had been placed there when Elmo came back from a nearby function room. Following him was Derik. It was nighttime and hours after the three of them first gathered and made the conversation in the same spot.

"It's trouble now. The Iraqis are lording it over toward everybody here in Kuwait, Tanya," Elmo commented.

"You mean, all those soldiers are Iraqis?"

"They are. Everyone of them," it was Derik who responded.

"They're so many. Why are they here in the hotel, Elmo?" Tanya questioned.

"I don't know," Elmo shrugged. "Perhaps, they're going to convert this hotel into their new home.

There was silence for a while.

"You think it's still safe for us to return to our apartment unit?" Derik asked Tanya. "The couple occupying that room between yours and the one Elmo and I are renting have been away for a week and haven't returned, I guess. Our landlords might have been missing."

"I haven't slept there last night to give way to Myra and her boyfriend ..." Tina was not able to finish what she wanted to say.

It was Elmo who continued it. "They slept there last night and ... Do you recall what the sergeant said?"

Hush prevailed once more. An uncomfortable feeling gripped the three employees. It was then that the two privates arrived.

"Miss, the sergeant wants to talk to you," one of the privates addressed Tanya.

"The two of you prepare a juice drink for the five of us," the other ordered both Elmo and Derik. "One glass at Room 213, four at 212."

It was at 213 where Tanya was brought by the two privates. When the door leading to the room swung open, the view inside was immediately unraveled before Tanya's eyes. There was an elegant matrimonial bed singly adorning the room with a round table and two chairs beside it. The sergeant was already occupying one of the chairs when he motioned Tanya to take the other chair.

"You told me you didn't know the girl in the pendant, remember?" the sergeant queried Tanya who was shaken.

Upon hearing the question, the two privates simultaneously sought permission from the sergeant to leave which gladdened the latter. "Wait all four of you at 212. You'll have your turn later."

The smiles the two privates wore on their faces earlier in the day when they entered an apartment unit led by the now deceased lieutenant were the same smiles they sported when they got out of Room 213. When they entered Room 212 they were laughing.

"You've heard my question," the sergeant reminded Tanya when the two privates had left.

"Yes."

"Well…?"

Still there was no answer from Tanya. Her fear was total.

Suddenly, knocks were heard from the door.

"Open it," the sergeant commanded Tanya and the latter obliged.

"Derik?" she uttered, showing surprise upon seeing the valet.

"Four seasons juice drink for the sergeant," and the valet slowly stepped into the room and carefully placed a glass of the juice drink he lifted with his right hand from the tray which his left was holding.

"Derik …" Tanya uttered as the valet merely nodded at her and hurried away from the room.

The sergeant stood up, went to the door and locked it. Turning to Tanya, he pushed her and the latter fell, her back on the bed.

"You lied to me!" he pointed his finger to Tanya who was not able to get up. Her shocked eyes saw the sergeant starting to unbutton his uniform.

"Please … Don't harm me …" she pleaded as she maneuvered her feet to push herself further to the opposite edge of the bed.

"You said you didn't know the girl in the pendant. She is working in this hotel! An employee at the *Items Shoppe* we questioned told us so," the sergeant growled as he removed his upper uniform.

"No ... Please...!"

Having pushed his trousers down to the level below his knees, the sergeant threw himself on top of Tanya who resisted with all her might but she was no match to the soldier's strength. He was like an angry animal ready to prey on his victim. He got hold of her underwear and stripped the helpless Tanya of it. Her shrieking voice reverberated throughout the room but her resistance was rendered futile. She wanted to shout with all her voice but found it would be meaningless at all. When the soldier made a thrust after placing himself on top of her, Tanya saw her world crumbling down. And when her tormentor disengaged from her, she felt it was the end of her.

His designs having been rendered complete, the sergeant reached for his glass and imbibed the liquid content.

Outside the room, it was quiet. Minutes later, footsteps were heard ascending the stairs from the first floor. It was Elmo. He went direct to the door of Room 213 and turned the knob but it was locked. Suddenly, the door of Room 212 clicked open and Derik went out.

"They made a toast. They drank their glasses together," Derik told Elmo who was fronting the door of Room 213. He acknowledged the valet's message.

Elmo leaned on the door to listen intently for any sound inside. It was silent for a while. All of a sudden a scream was heard. Elmo's reaction was spontaneous. He immediately pounded on the door which thereafter opened. Exposed to his view was Tanya in a wretched situation who pathetically embraced him and whom he tightly welcomed with both arms, pressing his lips on her tender cheek as an expression of pity and sympathy. He shared her grief. Derik was at Elmo's back, bewildered.

It did not take long for their attention to be drawn to the sergeant who was sitting on the chair with his head resting on the table. His mouth was frothing.

"I thought at first he simply had gone sleepy. Why then does he seem lifeless now?" Tanya asked.

"Derik poured rat poison on their drinks," Elmo told her. At his back, Derik nodded.

Tanya's eyes widened. In a moment she became frantic.

"Let's hurry, oh …" Tanya, momentarily unmindful of her situation strode outside of the room. "Let's get out of here, now."

The three of them descended through the stairs, almost running, and at the same time skirting the places where they would be visible to the soldiers. They went straight to the stock room of the hotel and searched for empty boxes and spaces where to insert themselves with nil chances of being located.

Less than an hour later, there was pandemonium in the hotel. The soldiers were busying themselves with something that they themselves were unsure of. They were looking for someone whom they did not even know.

The soldiers searched every nook and alley of the hotel. One even went to the extent of destroying the locked door of the stock room and focused his sight on what was stored therein. He kicked some boxes and, convinced that they were empty, he left. He nearly touched those where Elmo and Tanya hid themselves. In the space between two cabinets juxtaposed with other items in the corner of the room, where some goods were stacked, Derik was almost breathless as the Iraqi soldier's search was going on.

Minutes after the searchers left, no sound was heard anymore and the three of them who were in hiding had perspired profusely. Perhaps, it was the untold fear which induced it or maybe the distressful situation that was difficult to bear. Elmo, who was the first to emerge from hiding, was unsure. He was followed by Derik who tried to whisk away sweat from his face and neck with both hands.

They noticed that it took longer for Tanya to extricate herself from the box where she had hidden. Elmo was unsure again—whether it was really strenuous to get out of there or she may have been so affected by what she had gone into in the hands of the slain sergeant that she had to remain moped in hiding. Out of pity, Elmo extended a hand to her that she may be disengaged from the box. He was sure she may have been weakened by their daunting predicament which, on her part, was doubly unnerving.

"For how long have we been in hiding in your estimate?" Tanya asked her two companions.

"More than an hour, I think," it was Derik who answered.

"Where are they now?" she further asked.

The two men looked at each other. Then their eyes looked around and ultimately landed on Tanya who was also staring at them, wide-eyed. They were stunned by the unusual tranquility which pervaded the hotel.

"Let's look around. Slowly. . ." Derik suggested.

They stealthily moved out of the place where they had concealed themselves and tiptoed toward the end of an alley which could give them a full view of the lobby.

Suddenly, the loud noise of a revving engine jolted them. It was followed by more roaring ones. This sent them scurrying to the side door of the hotel and the full view of all military vehicles pulling away captured their eyes. They could hardly believe what they were seeing.

When the quietude of the surroundings was regained, an eerie stillness of the night confronted them. All the vehicles were gone except the service van assigned to Elmo for driving by the hotel management. Seeing it parked, he immediately ran toward it as Tanya and Derik followed.

They embarked on the vehicle almost at the same time. Elmo positioned himself at the driver's seat while Tanya sat beside him. Derik occupied the backseat.

"Where's the key?" Tanya panicked upon seeing that there was none inside the van.

"Relax, I'm the driver of this vehicle. It's with me," Elmo assured. He pulled out the key from his pocket and in an instant the engine started. With few maneuvers, the van began to deliver them outside of the hotel gate.

They were not yet too far when a deafening explosion made them quiver. Elmo applied the brakes and they turned their heads back. What they saw sickened them. The second floor of the hotel was burning. Another blast occurred and flames splurged in the third floor. Elmo stepped on the accelerator and the van zoomed away from the area.

"No, no..." Tanya wailed as she found that the sudden turn of events was simply too much to bear. She rested her head on the shoulder of Elmo who was doing what he could to maximize the velocity of the van he was driving.

Unexpectedly, a sound from a siren was heard. Derik turned his head and Tanya did too. They saw a military vehicle catching up with them.

"They're after us! Oh, my God. Elmo, let's get away!" Tanya found it hard to control herself. She was almost screaming.

Elmo jammed his foot on the accelerator lifting his vehicle's momentum. His military stalkers continued to tail them. When they were about to approach a junction, Elmo stepped on the brake, producing a sharp sound, and veered to the right. The military vehicle likewise did.

"Another one!" It was Derik now who shouted. He became worried as another military van joined the fray. There were two vehicles now tailing them.

Elmo concentrated on maneuvering the vehicle without failing to recall the considerations of safety. He had turned right twice already as there remained no letup in his drive to keep ahead of the race.

At the next junction, Elmo moved forward and the vehicle following him dashed, too. The last vehicle veered to the right. It was at the farther junction where Elmo made a turn twice with the first military vehicle still tailing him. At the next junction, the second military vehicle suddenly appeared and aimed to ram the hotel van. But the swiftness with which the van was manipulated by Elmo dodged the ramming car and it instead collided with the first military vehicle which was almost catching up with the van. The impact was so sudden and forceful that it sent both vehicles crashing. Elmo left them behind, the van's velocity not having been altered.

"Oh, it's dizzying," Tanya uttered as she held her head with both hands, whimpering.

They moved on southward, somewhat relieved, until they reached a crossroad.

"It's here where I get off," Derik announced, surprising both Elmo and Tanya.

"You're sure, Derik?" Elmo sought confirmation.

"Yes, it's the end of the line for me."

"But ..." Tanya could not find the words for Derik.

"From here I can walk to our country's embassy."

"Can't we take you there?" Elmo asked.

"No, you'll stir people. I'm better off walking to the place surreptitiously," Derik warned.

"Thanks for everything, Derik," Tanya said.

The valet just waved his right hand after having disembarked from the van.

***

Brian's awaited moment had come. He was apprehensive that the shadows of the night may turn out to be uncooperative to him, hence, he made a calculation that it had to be just before daybreak. His move had to be executed in clockwork precision as something may be lurking under the cover of darkness waiting to spoil everything he planned.

When he thought it was the proper time, Brian boarded a gray consular sedan which he availed of as his service vehicle whenever it was needed by the embassy for official purpose. He had a duplicate key of the said car. He started the engine and moved his vehicle slowly out of the gate of the embassy which he himself opened earlier. Some of those who had sought refuge at the embassy had awakened and were surprised at the sight of his vehicle being driven out of the area. Some followed him at the gate and, convinced that he was really leaving, closed the gate. He was not far enough when his eyes were focused on a vehicle stalled in the middle portion of the road. It either developed flat tires or had engine trouble.

Brian thus slowed down to make sure that there was adequate space left between the vehicle and a roadside post for him to get through. All of a sudden, knocks were heard coming from the side of his sedan. And when he moved his sight toward the source of the sound, he saw a woman waving her hand to signal that she wanted to board the vehicle.

"You?" he blurted out. Surprise made him do so.

She motioned again confirming her desire to be accommodated in the car.

Brian was curious at what she was up to. So he let her in. It was only then that he noticed she was not alone. There was another person, a man, who was with her and who did not show himself up first when she made the request to ride in Brian's automobile. The man took the back seat while the girl sat beside Brian.

"Please take me away from here. I need your help. I want to go home to Manila," the girl begged Brian.

"Please take me too. She needs my company. I shall not leave her alone till she finally gets home," the man likewise pleaded.

The DEWA was dumbfounded. The eastern sky was changing hue. There could not be any further delay. He had to rush.

"All right, all right," he then revved the car's engine and drove out of the place as speedily as he could.

Most of those who had sought refuge at the Philippine Embassy in Kuwait were still asleep, albeit uncomfortably and in any way they could, when he drove out of the compound—with the exception of those who had shut the gate after he left.

"This is a risky trip for all of us. But since I am convinced that you have a special case, we could take it as an exception. We'll try to reach Al Khafgie and proceed to Dhahran. The EWA in Riyadh will do the processing for you. You might join me in my search for someone," the DEWA told the girl after she had earned his sympathy.

The two were not strangers at the Philippine Embassy in Kuwait in the past. Brian could not have forgotten the girl's pretty face as he had seen her not just once before. At the hotel where she worked, Brian had attended functions several times. Brian took a very special interest at what the duo had narrated to him. The girl reported that she was raped by an Iraqi soldier inside a hotel room. The man who was her companion drove the vehicle out of the hotel together with her and another male companion, a valet who had since gone on his own. It was the same vehicle which got stalled near the embassy. He was told they were both working at the hotel.

"You said you had a co-employee who earlier escaped from the hotel, Tanya?" Brian asked. The speed of the car he was driving went steady at 100 KPH as soon as they were no longer in the city proper zone.

"Yes."

"What's her name?"

"Myra. Myra Castro."

"I don't think she ever sought refuge at the embassy."

There was silence for a while. Brian later said, "I think I met her once but can't recall having conversation with her. Unlike you ... We met several times and had talked to each other either twice or thrice."

"Yes, I recall. Maybe, it's because Myra was often in the night shift."

Brian nodded and concentrated on driving.

"No Iraqis on the road at this hour?" the man who had previously introduced his name to Brian as Elmo spoke.

"They're mostly in the northern part of the city. This is the southern portion. I think those who are stationed here are late risers. Good for us," Brian commented.

Words like those were sparse as the car they were riding continued to negotiate what appeared to be an endless highway to the border. Along the way they could see some abandoned cars.

Brian recalled what the couple had told him upon being accommodated in his car. He was taken aback at the realization of how Tanya's pulchritude had been wasted in such an outrageous, despicable spoilage.

The first makeshift border guards' station was now visible and Brian made a sudden stop.

"Why are we stopping?" Tanya wondered.

"I'll have to conceal Elmo in the car's hood. The two of us will have to pretend as husband and wife," Brian suggested.

Elmo did not expect it but he confined his amazement to himself. He humbly submitted to Brian's proposition. His concealment having been assured, Brian went back to the driver's seat. He reached for a small pillow at the back seat and gave it to Tanya.

"Insert this under your skirt," the DEWA said.

"Sir?" Tanya hesitated.

"It's necessary for our safety," he insisted.

Tanya was compelled to oblige. She lifted her skirt and inserted the pillow. As she did, Brian was able to notice the absence of underwear beneath her skirt. Tanya looked at him coyly.

"That dead soldier took it before he died."

Brian shook his head while Tanya rolled back her skirt, which she had been wearing as a uniform with her blouse since the previous day, toward her knees. As he took his eyes away from her lap, he noticed bloodstains on her skirt.

Later, at a considerable distance, they were headed to the first Iraqi soldiers' post. There were soldiers waiting. One uniformed guard signaled them to stop.

Brian unfurled some sheets of paper and showed the same to the guard with his identification card clipped thereon.

"Diplomat, eh?" the guard peered at him with piercing eyes.

"Yeah."

"Your wife's pregnant, sir?" the guard moved his dagger eyes to Tanya who quailed at the sight of a uniformed soldier.

"Sure."

The guard roughly folded Brian's papers and turned toward the direction where they were headed.

"Go," he said, handing back Brian's papers to him.

Brian lost no time in spurting ahead. There were even more soldiers at the second checkpoint as they approached it. It was supposed to be second to the last since they were already nearing the edge of Saudi Arabia.

Instead of stopping them, however, a guard merely motioned for them to proceed. It appeared that the soldiers assigned to the second checkpoint were either weary or had sleepless night before. Their movements characterized their being in a state of stupor. Anyhow, they were confident that the guards in the previous guarding post did their jobs very well so that the passage of motorists in their area would not be much of a concern to them. Their presence there may be taken as mere formality.

Coming to what appeared to be a third guardhouse, they saw the unexpected. The checkpoint was not manned. There was no trace of the soldiers around. Brian immediately took advantage of the situation. Their absence was to his delight. He drove the car as fast as he could and found no time to let Elmo resume his comfortable position inside the car. Brian was oozing with joy and excitement.

"Look, Saudi Arabia's gaping mouth is ready to assimilate us. You're now moving away from the claws of fear," he told Tanya.

It was not going to be so, however. When Tanya turned her head she noticed a vehicle tailing them. *And it was a military vehicle!*

"Look!" Tanya shouted.

Brian lost no time in looking at the side mirror of his car. He instantly recognized an Iraqi patroller.

"I wonder where they came from. They were not in their post when we passed by," Brian commented, worrying but driving his car in the fastest way he could.

"Maybe they came from the desert? Weren't they hiding there?"

"Maybe. We're in the border now. I can see the Saudi patrol cars ahead!" Brian exclaimed.

A thud at a certain point beside her perturbed Tanya. "They're firing at us!"

"Duck, Tanya, duck!"

Sirens then blared. Three Saudi patrol cars rushed toward their opposite direction. Brian applied the brakes and turned his eyes to the pursuers of their attackers who did not proceed far enough as they could not go beyond the border. It was then that he got to his senses.

"Elmo!"

Brian and Tanya swiftly disembarked and scurried to open the hood.

"Eeeeeeh!" Tanya shrieked as the bloodied body of Elmo was unraveled before her eyes.

Chapter Seven

It was an unusual and mystifying daylight which unfolded before Derik's eyes as he positioned himself astern on board a decrepit boat overloaded with mostly Sri Lankan nationals joined in by a few Indian and Bangladeshi citizens who were being repatriated to their respective countries on orders of the Iraqi authorities. Derik learned that their respective countries had requested the government in Baghdad that they be allowed such recourse and to facilitate such request, the Iraqis consented to a single option—that the repatriates would have to be conveyed by boat from the port of Kuwait City to Basra and from there a bus would take them to the Jordanian capital for a journey home.

"You're going home, too?" a man seated beside Derik, whom the latter calculated to be older than him by a couple of years or more and unmistakably a Bangladeshi, asked the valet.

"No choice, really."

There was no follow-up question from the man. An interlude of silence ensued and it gave Derik the opportunity to reminisce a chance occurrence he was able to get through with after his split with Elmo and Tanya hours before.

Trudging the road leading to the Sri Lankan Embassy from the point where he was left off by his two co-workers in the ill-fated hotel, Derik spotted from a distance that the road was being blocked by a group of Iraqi soldiers; thus, instead of proceeding he walked away and stood by at a road junction. Later, a 6x6 army truck with passengers cramped inside passed by and made a turn at the junction. He took the opportunity by hopping onto the passing truck which slowed down as it maneuvered through the junction, his hands grasping a railing on the side of the truck and his feet seeking at once the running board. Luckily for him, two of the Iraqi guards were seated with the driver in the front seat while the other two were deep inside the vehicle. It was during their disembarkation at the pier when a problem cropped up. One of the guards may have doubted his being a bona fide passenger in that truck, hence, the gun-slinging Iraqi questioned him.

"Are you really one of the legitimate Sri Lankan transferees for this trip?"

"I am."

"Hey," the guard called for an aging Sri Lankan passenger. "Tell me if what he'll say is a correct translation in your language."

Certain words in English were mumbled by the guard which Derik immediately translated.

"Was his translation correct?" the guard asked.

"Perfect," said the aging man.

Derik's abstraction was cut off when the man beside him uttered some words again.

"I'm not supposed to be on this trip."

"Pardon?" Derik asked him.

"I was slated for last night's trip."

"Why weren't you able to make it?"

"I was about to go on board ... it was a newer, bigger boat. Then two policemen arrived with four women, and one of them stopped the last four of us from boarding, saying we'll have to wait for the next schedule—in the morning. Our slots were given to the four women," the man turned melancholic.

"I see...."

"Those four passengers were Filipino women," the saddened man said.

***

The unraveling was too much for Tanya. She collapsed and almost fell to the ground were it not for the timely reaching out of Brian's arms to her to stave off an impact between her body and the hard pavement over which she stood. The DEWA immediately loaded her into the sedan and drove off to the nearest hospital, escorted by the Saudi border guards' vehicle. He no longer was able to remove Elmo from the car's hood as time was of the essence. On the way, an ambulance met them and the two patients were transferred into it.

When Tanya regained consciousness, she was already lying in a hospital bed, garbed in patient's attire and had all the medications ready to be applied to her should a need for the same arise. She momentarily looked around the room and found out she was alone.

Not long after, Brian and a Filipina nurse entered the room—they were in a somber mood.

"With all the tests completed and barring some complications, the doctors may pronounce her discharge in a day or two," the nurse was telling Brian.

"How's Elmo?" Tanya asked, finding a difficulty in doing so.

"I'm sorry, Tanya, he was pronounced dead on arrival," Brian dolefully revealed.

***

Alan rubbed his eyes and was initially clueless as to his whereabouts and on what was happening to him. He assembled his thoughts slowly and began reconstructing the dizzying events of the preceding day. He found it difficult to believe what he had gone into. He looked around after recuperating from the annoyance that suddenly struck him when he regained consciousness and turned upset, finding himself inside an abandoned warehouse. His leftovers scattered beside the pile of boxes used as containers of various goods over which he spent the night sleeping. He fed himself from what remained in his previous night's consumption.

Minutes later, he heard roaring sounds. He crawled to get nearer to the roadside and saw a tank and three armored vehicles carrying Iraqi soldiers passing by. He instantly hid himself behind the burnt structures and peeped through a crevice as the vehicles left the area.

He breathed heavily and planned what course of action to take. Things began pouring in his mind and his imagination stirred him to the occurrences back home. Tina must have been thinking about him—*and surely worrying, as who wouldn't be in this incident of global magnitude?*

Indeed, in Manila at that precise time, a throng had gathered around a building, and most of the people who were there showed distress, others were tormented. There pervaded an air of agitation as they crowded the frontage of a building where a hanging sign identified it as the home office of the *Stripes Shipping Corporation.*

It was the morning of the fourth of August in Manila and news of what sprung up in the Middle East had spurred them toward this building, hungry for news and wanting to ascertain how their loved ones were affected by the recent crisis.

Among those in the middle of the crowd was Tina, carrying a baby boy, less than a year old.

As the mood which permeated the crowd heightened to that of a disquiet, Tina could no longer conceal the signs of anguish running through her well-contoured face. Seeing a man who had just emerged from the door of the building, she approached him.

"What's the latest from there, please?"

"The ship's definitely in Kuwait."

"How about its crew?"

"No news on them."

"Why? Can't they contact them?"

"Contact with them is simply not possible."

As the man straddled to leave the area, Tina went on being relentless with him. "Anything regarding the other workers there … in other establishments, hotels … for example?"

"They can't even track down their own people," the man exasperatingly responded.

The man left while Tina stayed behind, feeling helpless and disconcerted, while tears fell down her cheeks as she cuddled her offspring.

***

Captain Villar looked over from the flying bridge where he stood and saw the men of Major Qassif getting too busy with the loading of cargoes on board the *M/V Hope*. Heavy crates and boxes were being transferred from military trucks to the vessel. The loading operations were carried out pursuant to the captain's instructions as he closely supervised the activities from his standpoint. Major Qassif, meanwhile, maintained a watchful eye as he also watched from the side of the ship facing the pier.

The captain observed that the new complement he was dealing with consisted not only of Iraqi nationals but also of some Palestinian volunteers and North African seamen.

After a while, the captain stepped away from the flying bridge and went to where the major was situated.

"This loading operation will take time," Villar told Qassif.

The major uttered no response. He simply touched his chin with his right hand as he continued watching the loading of crates and boxes into the ship.

***

After brooding for quite a time in his hiding place, Alan decided it was time to move out. He did not carry anything and walked casually as he trudged the sidewalk when a vehicle zoomed beside him and abruptly stopped ahead of him. He found out it was a police car. It was too late for him to make any move as the car drove back to his side.

One of its two occupants, the other one being the driver, got off and asked him.

"What were you doing inside that burnt compound?" The guy was a police corporal. Alan could identify him through the insignia he wore.

"Sir?"

"You seem to have just come out from that compound...."

"I had to pee. It was the most convenient place...."

"You're a Filipino?"

"Yes."

"Come with us."

"Sir, I'm on my way to the Qasrah Regal Hotel. I'm meeting my fiancee's sister there. She's employed in that hotel," Alan tried to ward off the invitation.

"That's still far from here. Ride with us. We'll take you there," and the corporal pointed to the back seat of the patrol car.

Alan was not able to pursue with his protestations anymore. He opened the door and took a step to the backseat.

"By the way, I'm Corporal Ubaud. Kuwaiti police," the man in brown uniform introduced himself.

***

When he opened his eyes, Peter Singh found that he had just come forth from a mental blackout. He had no idea where he was and wondered whether he was still with people on earth or had progressed to another life. He could still feel the pains in his body.

"You were unconscious when we loaded you in our vehicle. They dumped you body on the roadside, thinking maybe that you were finished," a man talked to him. From the way he looked, he would not be less than fifty. There were two other younger men with him.

"We're administering medications to ensure you recuperate fast. I'm a nurse previously employed in one of the clinics in this city," one of the younger men told Peter.

"We are members of the *Karalim*," the other younger man said.

Karalim?

Peter started asking more questions.

***

"You came all the way from the Philippines?"

The question from Police Corporal Ubaud lifted Alan from a reverie which was preoccupying him in the backseat of the police car. They had negotiated a considerable distance from the spot where the two police officers had picked him up earlier and Alan was at a loss on how to think right. *Was his decision to go separate ways and pursue a different destiny from that of the other dislodged seamen a correct one?* He was further musing: *what if the other sailors' relief from* M/V Hope *was a perfect move after all? Shouldn't he regret the precariousness of the situation he was in now?*

"Yes." It was all that Alan had to utter.

"I have a Filipina girlfriend. She's a nice girl."

"Where's she now?"

"She's on her way home."

"Did she abandon you?"

"No, I convinced her to go back to your country."

"Why?"

"She's no longer safe here. There's no guarantee we can hold on to our lives in the coming days," the corporal plaintively opined. "I'd rather prefer that she stay away alive than be at my side—lifeless."

Alan paused, then spoke to the Kuwaiti again. "Your surname is French sounding."

"My father's a Frenchman married to a Kuwaiti," Ubaud clarified.

"I see."

As their conversation had ceased, Alan concentrated on the vista and sights they passed by. He closed his eyes, expecting that out of the blackness, his mind might be relieved of those burdensome choices to make.

"This is where you're bound for," the stentorian voice of the car driver prompted Alan to open his eyes and immediately disembark from the vehicle.

At that precise moment he could not believe what he was seeing. The grandiose façade of the hotel he had visited was gone. In its stead, rubbles and charred skeletons of the once imposing structure punctuated the area, unraveling the annihilation of luxury the place in previous times was associated with.

"Oh ... no...!" Alan shook his head in disbelief.

***

Peter was told that the *Karalim* was made up of men and women, Kuwaitis and their sympathizers from other countries, who had formed an underground movement in Kuwait to fight the Iraqis and, although the organization was still in its fledgling state, it was growing. Peter thus became the newest recruit of the Kuwait Armed Resistance and Liberation Movement which carried the acronym of *Karalim*.

"Are you ready for the fight?" the man in his 50's asked Peter.

"I am."

"Good."

"I'm not new to this. As a midshipman officer way back in my days at the maritime academy I had trained for an activity akin to this. I was a naval reserve officer trainee and had learned a few tactics in the use of guns and in battle preparations. I'm a karate and judo enthusiast, too. I think I'm at home in this activity," Peter told the resistance fighters. His new role in a different undertaking had fascinated the seaman.

Peter's hands clasped with those of the other members. He observed that more men had appeared in their hideout. He now inevitably had become part of the resistance movement.

***

"I've got a proposal for you," Corporal Ubaud said to Alan without leaning back his head toward their passenger in the police car who had been grossly affected to the point of emaciation by what he saw in the premises of the erstwhile grand hotel.

"Corporal…?"

It became apparent to the Kuwaiti police officer that their passenger had his mind somewhere else. He repeated his utterance.

"What is it?" Alan sought for the details.

"Since it's certain you've got nowhere to go to, why don't you join us?"

"Join you?"

"We'll hire you as a civilian employee in our police unit," it was Ubaud's partner, the patrol car driver, who interjected.

"Are you serious?" Alan could not help but get awed by the proposition.

"Of course we are. You must know that although we fly Saddam's flag in this vehicle, it's only for show. You'll find Iraqi soldiers manning our station with us, but we're collaborating with them only as pretense. Truth is, we are their enemy. We want you to be on our side," Ubaud explained.

Alan's mouth dropped open.

"You've got to earn a living. Do it by killing them one by one," the driver said, drifting his car and making a left turn afterwards.

Part 3:
Loss of Hope

Chapter Eight

From the interior of the wheelhouse where he was standing, Captain Villar, who was positioned beside the helm, gazed at a far distance beyond the ship holding his binoculars and occasionally looking through them. He noticed that the pier premises were already cleared of cargoes and stockpiles had been removed.

Major Qassif, followed by six of his men, came out of a building in the harbor area and went straight to the gangplank to board the vessel. He looked up towards the sky before making the fist step onward to the ship and found that it was a fine morning of the fifth of August.

Upon getting on board, the Iraqi major proceeded to the bridge and, finding the captain there, told the latter: "Loading has been progressing rapidly."

"Yes," the captain spoke without turning his head to the major who was positioned at his back.

"Good. You said the loading would take time. It wouldn't be so."

Villar put aside his binoculars and faced the major.

He asked him: "Are you sure the remaining freight stacked down there are all you've wanted laden on board?"

"There's nothing else," Qassif answered.

"You haven't told me where they'll be unloaded."

"I'll tell you when the ship sails," the major snapped back, appearing irritated.

"Do you think they'd let us through?"

"What do you mean?"

There was no immediate response from the captain. The major looked at him intently, as if searching for a clue as to whether the ship master was taunting him.

When Villar finally did, he made his point. "The US and its allies. From our radio, it's definite now that they have imposed an embargo against your country. They'll turn back this ship once they know it's your cargo on board."

"They would not know! We are not afraid of them. We will not be cowed by them even if they should know. No one's going to stop this ship once it starts to sail!" the major stressed with a raised voice.

The captain showed no reaction to the major's rising temperament. He was unfazed. Hush prevailed for a while; then the major roared again.

"I want you to change the name of this ship!"

"What?!"

"You heard me."

Villar had not expected what he heard from Qassif. It was his turn to become enraged but found it an imperative move to control himself. He turned his eyes from the major for a while, and then faced him once more.

"What name do you want for it?" Villar's voice was now moderate, resigned to submission.

"I want the ship named after our city."

"*M/V Baghdad*?"
"Yes."

***

It was a huge edifice which caught the attention of Tina, who was still cuddling her son, as she sauntered through the sidewalk of a busy street in the central district of Manila. Its several floors housed the different private offices and business outfits along with some of the detached government entities, the most prominent of which was the *Middle East Coordinator's Office*—an agency attached to a commission under the Office of the President. The *MECO* occupied the fourth storey of the building.

A sleek black limousine was speeding toward the edifice and made a sudden, full stop when it reached the portion of the side street fronting the main door of the building. A ranking government official clad in dark suits disembarked followed by an aide and rushed to the elevator which would take him from the ground floor to his office in the fourth floor.

Tina followed the path he took. Reaching the fourth floor, she looked around her. A four-letter word, made up in strange font, immediately caught her attention: *MECO*. It was fastened to a slot just above the glass door leading to the interior of the office which directly faced the elevator door. Tina followed the other persons who entered the office. A female security guard was standing near the door, studying the profiles of individuals visiting the office, and it was she whom Tina approached first.

"Good morning, ma'am, may I inquire…?"

"Regarding what?" the lady guard snapped.

"Kuwait. I ... my . . ." Tina found it difficult to make known her purpose for being in that office.

"To him. You go to him," the blue-uniformed guard pointed to a bald-headed man holding office at the left corner of the area. Men and women of various ages were lining up towards his office table.

"Thank you," Tina addressed the guard.

"Welcome, but...."

"Yes...?" Tina was surprised at the additional word from the guard.

"I'm not sure if there's something you can get from him. I saw others earlier who, after talking to him, left shaking their heads."

Tina stood immobile for a while, then said: "Thanks, anyway."

She then joined the line formed by those who wanted words from the bald-headed man.

***

Two of Qassif's new recruits serving as ordinary seamen were on the verge of finishing their tasks on orders of the major. They covered the letters M-V-H-O-P-E at the ship's starboard and port sides with white paint and superimposed on the spaces the letters M-V-B-A-G-H-D-A-D. Captain Villar just stared at the men as they did their jobs. He felt resigned and helpless.

The captain turned his attention away from the men painting the ship's side and prepared to enter the bridge when Major Qassif approached him. The captain met the major with a question.

"Are you not courting disaster with what you've done?"

The major raised his eyebrows. "What do you mean?"

"By renaming this ship, you have just made it easily identifiable to your enemies."

"Hah! So what if they know that this is my ship. I am not afraid. I told you that before."

"Your ship?"

"Mine! Including all aboard it."

The fool! You'll realize what's yours in due time. Captain Villar wanted to confront the Iraqi major with the inanity of his combative posture but realized there was no way he could surmount Qassif's stance of haughtiness.

"They'll tail you to the edge of the world."

"It will be the end of them, mind you."

The captain relented and a brief hush ensued.

"What time are we sailing?" the major asked.

"I don't know," Villar answered nonchalantly. He shifted his sight to the wharf.

"What do you mean you don't know?" Anger and frustration showed in the major's face.

"We can't," the captain explained calmly. "The chandler hasn't arrived yet."

"What?! Damn, why didn't you tell me about it before?" Qassif turned riotous.

"You didn't ask."

The major walked a few steps away from the captain and turned back to him, growling and acting as if he would hit the master, but ultimately withdrew.

"Do we have to wait for that chandler?"

"We can't go to sea without provisions. It's simply impossible to sail without food and supplies. We'll all starve to death before we reach our destination," the captain explained.

"Then, get that chandler and let him come over to this ship quick!"

"If he's still around. With what you've done to Kuwait, there may not be a single chandler left in this place to tend to our needs."

Qassif cast a sharp look at Villar. If such look could render a slice, the captain would have been shredded to pieces. No words were exchanged between the two for some moments. The major turned away as he came into realization and thought about it when something instantly occurred in his mind.

"If we can't get it here, then we'll get it from Baghdad. There will be an oversupply of provisions in this ship. What the chandler here in Kuwait cannot provide, the government of Iraq can! Anyway, we can wait. This ship may not need to be in a hurry."

And the major began to laugh again.

***

"Thank you," Tina's expression of gratitude was sincere notwithstanding the fact that there was really no fruitful consequence with her efforts in making consultations with the bald-headed man pointed to by the lady guard.

"Welcome," the blue uniformed guard who was browsing a logbook on a small table where she was seated behind acknowledged Tina with a subdued smile, as if to send a message: *I told you so*.

"May I take that seat for a while?" Tina sought for the lady guard's permission when she noticed a vacant chair fronting the small table.

"Sure."

Tina sat down, placed her son on her lap and took out a half-filled feeding bottle to nurse her offspring. Meanwhile, the lady guard scribbled a note on a small piece of paper and gave it to Tina who did not expect it.

"Why don't you try that office…? Most of those who came here went there next," she suggested, handing over the note to Tina.

"So nice of you… I'm grateful…." And Tina gave her a more profound smile.

It was high noon when Tina stood up to leave the premises. The lady guard likewise stood up, stiffened her body while her right hand gestured for a salute and addressed a man who was passing by.

"Good day, sir!"

Tina saw a man in a hurry to leave the office. He was the same man she saw earlier: clad in dark suits, followed by an aide and had a sleek black limousine for his service vehicle.

"That's the Coordinator. He's leaving for Saudi Arabia," said the lady guard.

***

The police substation in the southwestern portion of Kuwait City was well-lighted in the evening of that day, as it had always been, although it was housed in a small bungalow-type structure and manned by a small complement. There was usually a dearth of matters to be acted upon brought before it.

Alan was earlier told by Corporal Ubaud that this could be due to the limited jurisdictional area it covered or there was actually no high demand for police action in places within its scope. Alan further surmised that no criminals had thrived in the area as the Iraqi soldiers were quite quick on the draw when it came to curbing criminality. *In fact, the criminals were no longer roaming the streets, they had joined the police in the latter's precinct.*

"Who's he?" an Iraqi soldier inquired upon Corporal Ubaud when he saw Alan serving them coffee.

"He's our new recruit—as a civilian employee," the Kuwaiti police corporal informed the soldiers.

Alan did not say anything and endeavored to remain silent at all times in the presence of the soldiers. Tonight there were four of them who had joined the police, the latter having the same number of personnel. Aside from Ubaud and the driver, there were two other PFC's in the post. Alan was earlier told that every night a different set of Iraqis joined the police in the act of overseeing the substation. They also differed in number: the least was three and seven was the most. Meanwhile, the two private first class officers, Alan noticed, were as silent as him. It was the driver-companion of Ubaud who did most of the talking. He and the latter were of the same rank and Alan knew him only lately as Corporal Menilli. It amused Alan to note that whereas Ubaud sounded as real French, his companion was resonantly Italian.

The soldier who had inquired about Alan stood up unexpectedly and went straight to the backdoor seeking for a place where to relieve himself. Menilli walked after him and signaled for Alan to follow.

When they were outside, Menilli took out a handgun and handed it over furtively to Alan.

"Shoot him," he said in a whisper.

"What?"

"Hurry up...."

Alan raised the handgun and squeezed the trigger. The soldier was hit in the neck and fell to the ground. Menilli pulled out his caliber .45 service firearm which was tucked in his waist and shot at the side of his left arm.

"We're being attacked...!" he whooped. Then he took back the handgun from Alan.

All those inside the substation were agitated and rushed outside. They saw the Iraqi soldier sprawling on the ground while the Kuwaiti corporal was holding his bleeding left arm. Alan was standing with a disconcerted face and had remained immobile.

"Hurry! Let's take him to the hospital!" almost all of them chorused.

"I'll remain here! Tincture of iodine can take care of my arm," Corporal Menilli declared.

All the Iraqi soldiers took off accompanied by the two PFC's to take their wounded comrade to a hospital.

"Your handiwork?" Ubaud sought confirmation from Menilli after the three of them were left in the substation.

"Yup, Alan's baptism of fire."

There was silence for a while.

"We're in trouble. It appears you did not finish off the target," Ubaud ominously uttered.

Chapter Nine

Their second night had been spent and it was worse than their first as the dislodged group of seamen from *M/V Hope* arrived at the consensus that it indeed was, while pondering on what sort of further misfortune may be in store for them in Baghdad as their captors awaited orders from higher Iraqi authorities. They had been herded into an army camp, as hostages, after arrival in the capital the day before and were given sleeping quarters in the barracks that the soldiers did not use anymore as there were new structures built which provided better comfort to the occupants. It was almost midday of the sixth of August.

"Are we better off than the three who didn't make it here?" the third mate attempted to draw comment from those who were gathered around him, some of whom were meditating while others stared blankly at those whom they were faced with.

"Are you referring to the captain, Alan and the sec…?" the quartermaster sought clarification.

"Who else?" Ben Gomez snapped.

"Ah, dear Ben, we are."

"It's no time to jest, Arthur," the third mate stressed a point to the QM.

"I'm not jesting."

It was time the chief mate said something, and he did. "I think Arthur's right. I am particularly worried for Alan. The captain stays with his ship wherever it goes and Peter knows his way around. But Alan...?"

"Where could he be ... now?" Ben asked.

"I think he was still there in the pier when we left," Chief Mate Eldon Ramos surmised.

***

It was already after lunch when Tina was able to leave home for the purpose of trying her luck at the address given her by the lady guard. The entire morning was spent waiting for her cousin to arrive home so she could have someone with whom to entrust her boy. It was quite wearying bringing him around.

When Tina arrived in the address stated in the note she was holding, she found the situation there more confusing than the two offices she had gone to in the past couple of days. People were gathered in front of the building which was of Spanish vintage identified by a sign above its entrance door as: *Labor Standards Monitoring Office for Overseas Sailors*. The acronym was even more confusing: *LSMOOS*.

Tina struggled to get near an employee but she simply could not get through the crowd. Inside the office, tables and furniture were cramped with only a small number of employees manning the hall. With frustration overrunning her, she decided to withdraw and was about to move away when she saw a man passing by. She thought she knew him.

"Hey...!"

The man turned to her.

Tina immediately asked him. "Aren't you Alan's classmate?"

"Yes, I'm Dennis Nillos. Alan Blancaflor and I graduated from the academy together last year," the guy introduced himself.

"I can't get any information regarding him despite having tried hard enough. This is the third day of my attempt."

"You're on...."

"Yes. He's been away for thirteen months. We're supposed to wed when he flies home this December."

"Really? Well, as for me, I'm unattached now.... Come, I'll take you to the boss in the upper floor. I work here, you know."

"Is that so? Oh, I'm thankful," Tina joined her both hands and raised them as if in prayer.

As they negotiated the stairway, Dennis commented. "Red tape. That's always the problem bugging us in our transactions with government agencies."

"Uh-uh...?"

"That's true. Although I'm employed here, I still nurture the belief that they should consolidate their services to the seamen. I was able to board a vessel, in a similar fashion as Alan did after graduation, but I got off after six months. Couldn't stand the policy. Why, for example, don't they just create a single entity, say a department of maritime affairs, to handle all the seamen's concerns on welfare and employment?"

When they reached the second floor, an aging secretary ushered them in to the chambers of the boss upon seeing that Dennis was accompanying a lady guest. The grey-haired boss was even older than the secretary who had a perfect old-maid profile.

"Come in, Dennis. Any problem?" the boss glanced at Tina first and then questioned his subordinate.

"Thank you, Mr. Ruiz. This is Tina. She needs help."

"May I know what kind of help I can offer?"

"Alan's ship was supposed to be in Kuwait at the end of July. I want to know if it's still there and what's happening to it now," Tina pleaded.

Mr. Ruiz picked up a phone, dialed numbers and made instructions to be connected to someone until he got to talk to the person he desired to have contact with.

"Yes … so…? Uh … huh…?"

Tina and Dennis watched Mr. Ruiz intently. When the latter put down the phone he spoke in a downcast voice.

"Well … Sorry, madam, we can't get anything from Kuwait. Our source is only up to Saudi Arabia and we can't go beyond. We have to wait for further developments."

Tina sobbed and Dennis led her out of the boss' chambers.

"Thank you, Mr. Ruiz."

As the door closed, the secretary took out a handkerchief and rubbed her eyes with it.

***

Major Qassif's chandler arrived just before the twilight of August 6, 1990 and stevedores started the loading of provisions for food and other supply items needed for the impending voyage of *M/V Baghdad*. Captain Villar noted that the chandler's goods were in large quantities and more than sufficient to fill the needs of the vessel if he were to quantify the same on the basis of the original itinerary.

Both the major and the captain stood beside each other watching from the ship how loading was being carried out and progressed.

"More porters and deckhands are being added into the work force. There's no reason why loading could not be completed by tomorrow," Major Qassif commented, turning his eyes to the captain who was a few meters his left, standing and holding fast to the railing while gazing at the men below rushing the cargo operation.

"Perhaps," Captain Villar wryly replied.

"You're running out of reasons not to sail," the major uttered with a smile on his face.

"I guess so," the captain intoned, his voice hinting at total resignation.

"Then?"

"When the dark sets in tomorrow, we'll pull away from this port."

"Good."

"You told me before you'd reveal our destination the moment we start sailing. I think you can do so now," Villar decided to confront the major with the question.

"Okay, if that's what you want."

"So, where to?"

"Yemen. We drop part of the cargo there, then we proceed to South Africa."

***

"What happened to her, Grace?" Myra could not conceal her being on the verge of panic as she inquired about the physical condition of the nanny who had been instrumental in her having been brought to their present whereabouts.

"Isabel complained of a dry throat. Now she feels being weakened," Ubaud's girlfriend informed Myra.

"Make sure she gets adequate water."

"Okay, Myra."

"And ..." Myra turned to the other domestic helper who had been a constant companion of Grace. "Your air supply, Edna, please don't relent."

"Don't worry, Myra, I haven't got tired yet," Edna who was fanning at Isabel with the use of a torn piece of carton assured.

Isabel who was lying on a cot inside a makeshift tent had closed her eyes while trying to catch her breath. She was sweating profusely. That was not her situation when Myra left her a couple of hours ago to inquire from those who were knowledgeable as to their current plight.

An upsurge of emotion struck Myra. The turnover of events was too sweeping and had left her coping up with agonizing consequences. Days ago, she was in pure delight while locked in the arms of her boyfriend Peter and had comfortably relished the ambience of the luxurious hotel she was working in. Now, she was being housed inside a makeshift tent in the middle of the desert with her three lady companions who were as uncertain as she was on the kind of future they had to face—if there was any at all.

Myra got out of a tent and faced the horizon, a point where the sky and the sand met. There was no luster in the firmament as the nocturnal shift would soon be in place. Spotting the fading gleam in the horizon, her mind yielded doubts and worries. Was her decision to leave the embassy with her three female companions the right one? Or was it nothing but an ill-conceived, improperly weighed option? What if she just stayed put at the embassy? Wouldn't it have been a better alternative?

Reminiscences occurred in Myra's mind. The moment they boarded that boat in the Kuwaiti port, through the courtesy of Corporal Ubaud and his buddy, things would never be the same again. She could no longer recall how long it took them to reach Basra nor how far they traveled from Basra to nowhere—the place she had been brought into and now serving as her provisional homeland. *But for how long?*

When their boat was floating beside Peter's ship, and she had occasion to cast a furtive last glance at it, there was an unexplained feeling that visited her. She could not deny that she disliked that ship as it had always been the reason behind Peter's constant act of leaving her. *Indeed, every time it sailed it drew Peter away from her.* But at the last moment she saw it, she thought it was pitiable, deserved to be admired and praised. *Ah, that poor and forlorn ship!*

"Myra ..." Grace had called for her and Myra got back to her senses.

Darkness had taken over and the flickering lights were now visible all throughout the tent cities which had been set up in a wide strip of the desert between Iraq and Jordan to accommodate thousands of refugees from Kuwait wanting to be flown home to their respective countries of origin. It was here where Myra and her companions were brought contrary to their hope of being ferried directly from Basra to Amman where flights were readily available to take them back home.

"What's it, Grace?"

"The doctor is here."

The physician introduced himself to Myra. "I'm Doctor Khamadi from the Jordanian Medical Society. We've set up a volunteer medical mission to attend to the needs of sick refugees here. Just follow what's prescribed to be done in this note. And watch out for signs of dehydration."

"Thank you, doctor," Myra said after receiving the note from Doctor Khamadi.

Chapter Ten

A day after the shooting of an Iraqi soldier at the Kuwaiti police substation, which was widely bruited about as an assault on the precinct, seven Iraqi soldiers were assigned to guard the post and beef up the police complement on duty therein. Nightfall having taken over, Alan busied himself with the preparation of his brew for the consumption of their usual *guests*.

"The loyalists of the former ruler are resorting to guerilla warfare in order to scare us," Menilli voiced out a comment in the usual loudness characteristic of him. It was intended to be heard by all those around.

The seven Iraqi soldiers just nodded their respective heads, their lips unmoved.

"Better to be prepared," Menilli continued as he toyed with his machine pistol which was actually his ploy to assure himself that it was ready to fire.

The door leading to a portion of the substation which served as the pantry opened and Alan came into view. He was carrying a tray with several cups of steaming coffee on it.

After distributing the cups, Alan told his guests who did not receive their own share of the brew: "More cups are coming."

"I want a mug," one of the soldiers ordered.

"All right, sir."

Alan immediately disappeared upon reaching the door where he previously emerged. Before he could get back to serve more coffee, a loud screech was heard outside and a burly officer barged into the substation, followed by two aides, and confronted Ubaud. Some of the Iraqi soldiers snapped a salute while others failed as they held on to their cups of coffee.

"You're all liars here. This place was not attacked by marauders last night. You shot my soldier!" the officer growled at the same time placing his hand on his holster.

Menilli did not take chances. He sprayed the burly military official with bullets from his machine pistol. What followed was a shooting spree which cut down both protagonists. Alan saw it initially with his horrified eyes as he peeped through the jalousies separating his area from the substation's lounge. As the firing raged on, he ducked and stood up only after the shooting rampage had died down. He saw Corporal Ubaud as the last man standing.

"Quickly, Alan … Let's get to the patrol car!"

The two of them lost no time in running toward the vehicle, skipping over the bodies of those who had fallen: all the Iraqis, the two PFC's and Corporal Menilli.

Corporal Ubaud, after occupying the front seat with Alan beside him, forcefully maneuvered the police car from the scene and put on a burst of speed. As they hurtled through some narrow roads of

Kuwait City, wailing vehicles streamed into the police substation.

The car pulled up in the vicinity of the French Embassy and Ubaud queried Alan. "Do you know how to drive this thing."

"Yes."

"In that case, take this car away with you and find the safest place you can reach. There's nowhere else I could go."

And Ubaud abandoned the car to Alan.

After a considerable distance, the displaced seaman felt fretful inside the car. He stopped in one deserted street and relinquished it. He had walked not far enough when he heard the sound of an engine. He hid himself behind a post and later saw a military vehicle approaching; it stopped briefly beside the forsaken car and resumed speed. A loud explosion caused Alan to cower and when he regained his posture, he saw the car he left burning. He made rapid strides to leave the area and when he reached a corner, he stopped to obtain breathing space. Suddenly, he felt something hard and cold touching his nape. Fear grew within him as there was no mistaking that it was the nozzle of a gun.

***

"You have a visitor," the nurse who first attended to her when she was taken to the hospital where she now rested appeared in the door of Tanya's room and greeted her.

"Who?"

"Me, of course," Brian showed up, following the nurse.

"Thanks, Brian … So kind of you…." And tears began forming in Tanya's eyes.

"Relax, Tanya, you'll get by and surmount all these…." Brian sat down beside the patient and held her hands.

Tanya got up, leaned towards Brian and sobbed. She fell upon Brian's chest, her tears wetting the DEWA's shirt.

"You're due for discharge tomorrow. From here we will proceed to meet the Coordinator in Dharan," Brian told Tanya.

"Brian, I'm afraid…."

"Have no fear, Tanya, the Coordinator will take you home."

After a brief exchange of words with the nurse, Brian bade goodbye to Tanya.

"You're leaving too soon, Brian? I have no one to turn to now."

"You'll have one, Tanya, when you get back to the Philippines."

***

Alan initially intended to run but such impulse might not bring him any relief at all, thus, he was compelled to raise his both hands in surrender and slowly turned his head. A man, about his age was pointing a rifle at him while two other men surfaced from the dark, both armed with long weapons. The three men were Arabs. They led Alan across the road and passed through several passageways until they reached a cottage.

One of the armed men switched on a flashlight after he, Alan and the two other armed men entered the cottage. There were two more men already inside and they were the ones who took Alan away from his captors, bringing him to the back portion of the cottage. There was a room there which they went into.

A man was waiting inside. He lighted a small lamp since the room was dark and it produced a faint light revealing the perplexed face of Alan and also the man's face. Vibrations of shock clashed between them.

***

Tanya finished the meal which she left untouched prior to the coming of Brian. The latter's presence, even though how brief, was somehow reassuring as it provided relief to her otherwise agonizing sensibility. The words he imparted to her had the effect of bringing about a paradigm shift. *Was she really coming home?*

It really would be difficult to anticipate what consequences it would bring to her. She thought she had a customary life in Kuwait and she had nothing more to crave for at all. Except that she was loveless, unlike her best friend Myra who seemed to have come full circle in matters concerning the affairs of the heart. But to Tanya such thing could wait and may be tackled in the opportune time. There were several propositions from some guys before but she never took them seriously as she thought these were just fleeting fancies. The one which she deemed of substance came from Elmo but he was so subtle about it that she mistook the same for a mere admiration, an extended infatuation, and needed no substantial reciprocation from her—until the very last moments.

Home to where the heart beckons?

Tanya realized only now that she may have invested every aspect of her well-being to her job in Kuwait, including the exigency of her womanhood, that when the time to consider it came, a beast had unceremoniously pushed it to destruction. She was now in a dilemma as to how to recoup what had been extirpated. She was at a loss on whether it was still possible to put together once more her ruined life.

And what's in store at home?

She went to Kuwait because there was none in the first place. She and her younger sister Tina, with a year's gap in age, grew up in the care of an aunt who had a daughter of her own as they were abandoned by their parents at young age: their father went to Vietnam as a soldier and never came back. Not long after, their mother married another man, a Cambodian, and resettled with him in his country during the Pol Pot era. She left her younger sister Tina with her aunt less than two years ago when she was hired as hotel employee in Kuwait after finishing a two-year course in Hotel and Restaurant Management. Tina got impregnated by her boyfriend Alan who promised to marry her when his apprenticeship on board an ocean-going vessel would be over. Alan revealed this to her during the seaman's unexpected visit to her in the hotel where she was working in Kuwait City six days before that fateful night in a room therein, the memories of which jarred upon her even in sleep.

That visit of Alan gave her a memorable day in stark contrast to the repulsive night she went through at the hotel. It was an opportunity for her to make out a clear perception of the guy and evaluate whether her sister had discriminatingly assessed a potential partner in life. It happened that on such day, her duty was to start at four o'clock in the afternoon. She was at the hotel lobby, having just freshened up in the nearby apartment she shared with Myra, to assist the latter in fixing things up related to their work—at around nine in the morning—as Myra intended to apply for leave from work since her boyfriend was arriving that morning. Tanya was surprised to learn that Alan came together with Myra's beau.

While Myra was getting too excited to fall in the arms of her boyfriend, she and Alan had to entertain each other, as the lovers immediately became oblivious of them.

"You know what, Tanya? My boss can hardly wait to have your friend locked in his loving arms," Alan whispered to Tanya.

She was tickled on hearing it, so she whispered back: "I'm an understanding type, so I made arrangements with the hotel to spend the night in one of the quarters here. That way, the room I'm sharing with Myra in our apartment is theirs for taking."

As Tanya belatedly realized she should have withheld the information, both of them shared the laughter.

She again whispered to him. "This is only between the two of us."

"Of course. I'm not revealing this to anybody, not even to Tina." It was not laughter but a meaningful smile which they shared this time.

Tanya pinched Alan at the left side of his body. "Don't be a liar to my sister."

Alan squirmed, saying: "I wouldn't be … except if it comes from you."

And Tanya pinched him some more.

"You know what, Tanya?"

"What more?"

"The first time I saw you—as guest muse of our freshman team in the academy—I thought you were the kind of girl who's an introvert, uninterested in men, especially."

"And…?"

"It was a wrong impression I found out later. Truth is, you're fun to be with," Alan told her.

A sudden spate of drowsiness snatched Tanya from her recollection and minutes later her eyes closed and her body made no movements anymore. But before she did, a smile flashed across her face— the first time since that dreadful night in the hotel.

***

"Alan?!"

"Sec … Second Mate Singh?!"

The two sailors could not believe they were facing each other as the glow of light revealed their faces. After a brief astonishment and a confirmation of their having run into each other, they embraced and renewed their bonding.

"Sir Pete, I thought you've gone away for good. I never expected this contingency that would bring us together once more," Alan tearfully heaved out.

"Alan, when destiny is up to something, there would always be moments like this," Peter explained, holding both shoulders of his apprentice mate.

"And these are really moments to cherish, sir."

"You've got it, Alan. Now, welcome to *Karalim*!"

Chapter Eleven

The moment being waited for by the captive seamen in Baghdad appeared to have come in the morning of the seventh of August. As they continued to play their guessing game on what outcome would finally face them in such a situation, the camp that served as their temporary abode was stirred when the arrival of a certain high-ranking military official in the Iraqi armed forces with a column of siren-blaring vehicles escorting his chauffeur-driven limousine was announced.

"You form a line and salute the colonel the moment he passes by in front of you per instructions from Captain Ukuf," a sergeant instructed the seamen.

When the Iraqi colonel disembarked from his vehicle he went straight to a cottage being occupied by the camp commander.

"Will he be addressing us?" the third mate whispered to the chief mate who was right beside him.

"I think he will be giving out instructions on what to do with us," Chief Mate Ramos whispered back.

"Oh, my ... What would that be?" Third Mate Gomez suddenly turned apprehensive.

The chief officer merely exhibited a distorted facial expression indicating he was in no position to guess.

After a while, the colonel was seen getting out of the camp commander's cottage and proceeding to the venue occupied by the seamen who were lined up by their sides. As instructed, they rendered a salute when the Iraqi official passed by. The latter cast a momentary look at them and immediately withdrew.

The camp commander, Iraqi Captain Ukuf, waited for him as he turned back, and coldly asked a question.

"Sir, shall I line them up before a firing squad?"

Each one of the seamen heard those words exactly as they were uttered.

***

"Do you think you're well enough for the first mission?" the leader of the movement asked Peter and Alan.

"I am," the second mate confirmed.

"I am, too," Alan echoed.

"Good."

The leader took out a set of documents from a folder and handed over the same to Peter. Alan watched behind him. When the second mate started leafing through the documents, he noted that a map was appended to the file and he easily discerned it as charting the entire city of Kuwait and its outskirts.

"You haven't told me what your name is," Peter commented while scanning the documents.

"All of them call me *first*, meaning the first among equals. If I'll tell you my true name, you'll find no significance in it anyway and besides it's difficult to pronounce and may be incomprehensible to you."

"Well, thank you, Mr. First," Peter said.

***

"No!"

The camp commander found it difficult to attach a meaning to the colonel's reply to him.

"What then shall we do with them?" Captain Ukuf further inquired.

The beguiled seamen stared at each other, finding the turnover of events too abrupt, in contrast to the erstwhile sluggish predicament they had been cast into. The upsurge of fear that almost swallowed them up had quickly dissipated and instead they were made to hang in the balance as the colonel's clarification was being awaited.

"Release them. Let them board the earliest bus bound for Amman. These people deserve a prize in exchange for a vessel they abandoned in our favor which was simply what we needed in time. And it's what they'll get—freedom," the colonel stressed.

"Yes, sir, Colonel Ahfed, sir," the Iraqi captain obliged, executing a snappy salute as the colonel left him.

Incredible!

That was what the eyes of every seaman who heard the colonel's words conveyed to each other as their distressed looks turned to excitement.

***

Myra found consolation whenever she stood facing the extensive stretch of sand and staring at the point where it would meet the sky, sometimes streamlined by streaks of light, yellowish to occasionally reddish, to signal a shift from day to night. The woman she was watching over had been convalescing, to the betterment of her physical condition, and Myra believed she needed to refresh her own self with the gently slapping breeze, though at times vapid, outside their tent which smacked of discomfort.

Myra removed her sandals from her feet and used the same as sort of cushion to sit upon as she stretched her legs on the warm sand.

She had concentrated her thoughts on faraway places: the Philippines, Kuwait and how everything had boiled down to her present encampment. She had looked above her, at the distant sky and the faraway horizon, and when she lowered her eyes, she saw a creeper, larger than usual, which was crawling toward her feet. She was about to shriek when somebody's foot stomped on it and gyrated with the creeping thing as the axis until it cracked and granulated.

Myra raised her head to ascertain whose foot it was and it stunned her to find out.

"Derik?!"

"Yes, Myra, it's me."

"I couldn't believe it. How did you ever find your way to this forsaken site?" Myra moved upward, coming face to face with Derik.

"I, too, refused to believe it at first. I've been tailing you since this morning to find out if it's really you. I didn't show up until I was hundred percent sure."

"You came just in time."

"Come, let's sit down and you'll find out more from me," Derik held Myra's hand to stress the invitation.

"I'm afraid of scorpions!" Myra protested, pulling back her hand.

"They're no longer coming now that I'm here," Derik insisted.

Myra was swayed and she sat down beside Derik.

"After you left the hotel, the world turned upside down, Myra." And Derik commenced to narrate the harrowing occurrence from the arrival of the soldiers at the hotel until he left Tanya and Elmo in the vehicle driven by the latter.

Myra sobbed on hearing the narrative, and when it came to the point of Tanya's ordeal, she cried the loudest, resting her head on Derik's shoulder. The valet tried to console her, extending his right arm around her shoulder and touching gently with his left hand her cheek where the tears flowed, whispering to her: "Calm down, Myra, Tanya will get through with it."

When the tensive atmosphere had receded, it was already dark and Derik stood up, pulled Myra by the hand and guided her to the tent city which had put on lights.

***

Wrapped in an ebony milieu, the palely lighted ship slowly disengaged from the illuminated wharf after silent maneuvers and was soon absorbed by the mass of darkness, leaving the reflections of its lights upon the murky water as the only visible sign of animate existence in the area. As the harbor lights vanished, its velocity was enhanced and soon it was slicing its way through the infinite sea.

A clock in the bridge showed it was almost nine in the evening and Captain Villar started to feel somewhat relaxed after having been in command during the undocking procedure. Major Qassif, who had remained in the bridge, was sulking in contentment.

"You are expected to listen at all times to what I have to say and you should observe how the turnover of watch is done. Clear?" Captain Villar addressed a new member of the complement, a Tunisian seaman who had been designated to take over the functions of Alan.

"Aye, aye, sir!"

The captain then turned his attention to the major.

"At the speed of eighteen knots, we're well on our way to Yemen."

Major Qassif who was smiling nodded in approval. He observed that the captain made it a point to his new aides in the bridge that they had to learn the art of navigation the way Villar wanted it.

The guy who took over the job of Alan was a Tunisian seaman who had not yet earned a nautical license but assiduous enough to deserve it. He had Alan's industry and was almost perfect for the latter's job. He was, however, in a wrong place at a wrong time. How he got to join Qassif's complement was a puzzle to the captain, and his ambition to succeed in navigation under the prevailing conditions was even more perplexing. Iraq seemed to have recruited internationally people of divergent orientations to rally to its cause under promises of, perhaps, everything.

***

"Look at this!"

The naval technical assistant was unsure whether the words he blurted out with were self-addressed or directed to his stupor-prone immediate superior seated right behind him who was undeniably brooding. The ensign's attention was not being directed to the elaborate gadgetry highlighted by several monitors, the monotonous screens of which may have contributed to the moroseness getting to be a trademark of his personality, but to something else beyond the confines of their humming, sophisticated naval ship.

"What is it?" Ensign Dean S. Eaglewood came back to his senses after hearing Brent Brundy's jolting, high-pitched voice.

"It pulled out of Kuwait and initially maintained a steady course, then it veered, appearing headed straight to the Strait of Hormuz," Brundy's voice had a tone of excitement. The rhyme and rhythm were purely coincidental.

"Speed?"

"Moderately maintained. Perhaps stable at eighteen knots on steady course."

"Good. Keep an eye. A hard eye. Analyze with care and meticulousness the data being fed us by *Capricorn*," Eaglewood ordered.

"Aye, aye, sir!" Brundy perfunctorily uttered.

When he later turned his head to see what the ensign was up to, he found him back in the latter's usual way—uncaring, slouched in his chair and looking beyond the porthole at the side of their encasement. Brundy surmised that Eaglewood may be thinking about his wife and son back in Seattle. The ensign had previously disclosed that his son was only a three-year old boy and he never had any inkling that he would be given this assignment seven months ago. He was plucked from his office work in a unit at San Diego and given the task of commanding the Vital Relations, Exchange and Communications Section (referred to as the VRECS in the US naval network establishment), a specialized and advanced component of the nautical operations on board the *USS Alaska*—a modern-day version of a US frigate which was the latest addition to the American contingent in the Arabian Sea accompanying the aircraft carrier *New York*. The *Capricorn* served as their satellite source and connection.

Brundy assumed a relaxed posture but his eyes remained fixed on the screen he was facing.

Chapter Twelve

Captain Villar held his binoculars and looked at a distance through the instrument as the ship, *M/V Baghdad*, continued to prowl the vast sea. It was a clear and sunshiny day which greeted the eighth day of August. But deep within him, the spirits of gloom prevailed and provided a contrast between his outward and inward perceptions.

The captain's new aides in the bridge performed their navigational tasks in compliance with his instructions. The guy who took over the job of Alan, a Tunisian seaman, was seen by the master as an assiduous doer of the work assigned to him.

Villar was in the thick of musing when the door of the bridge opened and Major Qassif emanated from the outside. He was wearing a smile as each one of those who had noticed him instinctively rendered a salute. His entrance to the bridge was preceded by a momentary standing at the side of the deck and taking a breath of sea air.

"A nice day for navigating, isn't it?" the major sought for the master's like thinking.

"It sure is."

Qassif nodded.

"Why two destinations? Why Yemen first and then South Africa?" the captain asked the major after a lull in the exchange of words.

"You asked me of our destination last time and I told you. Now, you're asking why."

"If you won't mind."

"Well, I can tell you. You seem to have gone along with me. You're the captain, anyway. Perhaps, you deserve to know. You might join me in my pursuit."

"A pursuit of your own?"

"Come, you'll find the answer," Qassif motioned for the captain to join him outside the bridge in order that the former's puzzlement may be addressed.

"You take care," Villar instructed the helmsman as he followed Qassif who prepared to leave the bridge.

On the lower deck of the vessel, where crates were stacked and other cargoes stowed, a common sailor who was part of Qassif's complement welcomed his two superiors.

"These constitute freight of value," the major revealed. "Treasures and all. South Africa is an economic wizard and not difficult to deal with when it comes to matters of mutual advantage to itself and the proponent of the deal. These cargoes will land there."

"You've struck a deal with them?"

"Correct."

"And you stole these things from Kuwait?"

"Ah … ah…!" Qassif placed his right index finger upon his lips to come up with a sign for the captain to shut his mouth.

"You deal with those people…. You are an international racketeer," Villar went on.

"Ha-ha-ha-ha-ha!" Qassif, instead of getting mad, unleashed a guffaw.

"You are a thief from Baghdad."

Qassif cut his laughter abruptly upon hearing the statement from the captain.

"You say something more and you'll be dead sooner than you think!" he blurted out, at the same time pulling out his pistol from its holster and aiming at Villar's head.

The captain stepped back and turned his head away from the major. When the latter's outburst ebbed down, Villar continued asking.

"And the other cargoes for Yemen?"

"Fireworks! Great balls of fire from Yemen will incarcerate the Saudis and their allies. Ha-ha-ha-ha!"

As the major exploded in laughter again, the captain turned away from him in anger and frustration.

"Oh, my God!"

Qassif had one more query for Villar. "You'll join me in this business, won't you?"

The master uttered no word and withdrew from the major completely. The latter continued laughing as Villar left him behind.

***

When Brian and Tanya arrived in Dharan, Saudi Arabia, having proceeded there after the latter's discharge from the district hospital, the Coordinator was already waiting for them. Rustico Casabuena was in the prime of his diplomatic life at age sixty-two and had represented his country in various foreign missions culminating with the rank of ambassador extraordinary and plenipotentiary to Morocco. That was the last position he held prior to his current job as the Middle East Coordinator of the present-day regime in the Philippines.

The position of Coordinator was attached to the *Presidential Advisory on Foreign Relations*. The *Advisory* was headed by the Foreign Secretary with two other persons of consequence as members. In effect, the Coordinator served as the link between the President's consultancy council and the former's area of concern. However, the Coordinator's task was not merely in the nature of consultancy. Far beyond that, for he also served as an executor, an action man. He was his country's specialized functionary in his area of responsibility. As a matter of fact, the office of the Coordinator was in the level of a commission and the Coordinator himself carried the rank of a commissioner but each of the Coordinators had the preference of being referred to as such.

There were five Coordinators serving under the *Advisory*. Their assigned areas of concern were: the ASEAN region; North America and Western Europe; the communist and socialist states; South America, Africa and Australia; and the Middle East.

Each Coordinator tackled not only the diplomatic and consular matters consequential to the Philippines in his specific geographical assignment but also the employment and welfare aspect affecting Filipinos working in his domain.

Thus, Rustico Casabuena's preoccupation today bordered on panic and frenzy. A series of long distance calls from his men had sent him flying to Saudi Arabia as his office in the Philippines turned into an agitated hive. He had reason to be worried. His turf was on the spot.

And that was not all. His daughter Rose, who was Brian Rios' betrothed girl, worked as a resident physician in one of the hospitals in the troubled area.

"Sir, this is Tanya," Brian introduced his female companion to the Coordinator.

"Come, let's talk in the lounge." And the Coordinator led them to the place which he preferred, expecting a more relaxed, private and convivial mood as they prepared to tackle some sensitive matters. They talked about Rose first. Brian shook his head as he talked to the Coordinator whose face had turned sullen. Then they shifted their attention to Tanya.

"What happened to you should be kept under wraps back home," Casabuena's stoical but penetrating way of communicating to Tanya caused her uneasiness. "The matter of your having been raped should not be divulged but known only to us. What happened should never become an issue at home."

Tanya turned her eyes away from the two men. She tried to piece together the fragments in the Coordinator's mind while beginning to turn teary-eyed.

"This thing between Iraq and Kuwait is none of our country's concern. We have good relations with both of them. We should maintain a neutral stance in this present state of affairs. The countries concerned should settle their own dispute without necessarily involving third parties who proffer friendly posture. Premature revelation of an incident which has not yet undergone a thorough investigation may ruin that stance we are trying to adopt," the Coordinator emphasized.

Brian was sure he was treading the Coordinator's line of thought. He understood, more than anyone else perhaps, that Casabuena intended not to tilt the balance as he walked the political tightrope, both ends of which were tied to his own welfare, that of his country, and in a large sense, the world.

"Your papers will be immediately processed," the Coordinator assured Tanya. "Tomorrow you will be on a plane with me to Manila, via Amman, where I have to leave instructions and fix things before returning home."

He then turned to Brian. "You'll go back to your post. You'll return to Kuwait as soon as we have left."

***

Alan held firmly the Kalashnikov. Peter trained him to handle it, applying his own lessons gotten from the *Karalim* members who had shared with him their expertise in using the weapon. The rifle was confiscated by the resistance fighters from an Iraqi soldier whom they ambushed while on patrol a few nights before. Alan went with Peter and two other members of the group to a site near an abandoned radio station and positioned their bodies clandestinely at a wrecked portion of the building the media outfit once used—as therein they would be least noticeable.

Their waiting did not take long. Four Iraqi soldiers were walking in the vicinity. They ambled slowly toward them but their voices were loud. Bearing confidence, they walked past Alan's group.

With the soldiers' back on them, Alan positioned the Kalashnikov and aimed it at one of the soldiers. Peter and their two companions followed suit. They did the aiming with their respective rifles. It was man to man.

The sounds of gunfire reverberated throughout the streets branching from a nearby junction and perturbed an otherwise torpid night. The bodies of the four Iraqi soldiers simultaneously fell to the ground. They were lifeless. The four *Karalim* members rushed to retrieve their scattered rifles and ran swiftly under the cover of darkness. Their shadows merged with the murk of the night.

"Keep on running! It won't take long before their comrades will find out what happened to them," Peter instructed as their group inched through the branching passageways toward their hideout.

"Congratulations on your successful initiation in this undertaking!" Peter gave Alan a pat as soon as they were back in their safe-house.

Chapter Thirteen

Captain Porfirio Villar glanced at the clock hanging overhead in a portion of the bridge and the hands of the timepiece unmistakably told him—it was precisely midnight. They were on the verge of entering the ninth day of the month and almost a week behind their expected date of departure from the port of Kuwait.

A smile flashed on the captain's face but it was momentary, being soon effaced by a frown that further gave way to sullenness.

Meanwhile, Major Qassif was in deep slumber inside the owner's cabin. The luxurious furnishings of the most elegant room in the ship were but mute witnesses to the annoying snore of the major.

There were three persons in the bridge: Captain Villar, the Tunisian seaman and another sailor holding the wheel.

"You man the wheelhouse while I'm taking myself to the cabin. I'll be back in a while," he told the two deck assistants as he prepared to leave the bridge.

"Aye, aye, sir," the two chorused.

When Villar reached the master's cabin he donned his bush jacket, opened a tightly sealed steel chest and took out a jungle knife which he later inserted in one of his boots. His hands then groped for a grenade well kept in a portion of the chest and transferred it to a pocket of his bush jacket. Thereafter, he got out of the cabin and returned to the bridge.

"The Gulf seems calm and we're stable," he commented upon reentry to the bridge.

"Yes, sir," the helmsman responded.

Villar stared at the darkness outside the ship which to him was as void as the situation he was now in. A plan long hatched in his mind had to be implemented before their vessel would prowl beyond the Strait of Hormuz in the Gulf waters and deep into the Arabian Sea. This would be the opportune time. *It had to be now.* It would be for the good of *M/V Hope*, for himself and, perhaps, for all of them on board, including Major Qassif.

Captain Villar had previously wondered what freight was to be dropped in Yemen and what should be brought to South Africa. Now it dawned on him, after the conversation with Qassif, that the latter was a partner in an international racketeering syndicate with worldwide connections—particularly in Yemen and South Africa. Yemen was Iraq's ally and South Africa could engage in a deal if there was a promising outcome in it. The captain surmised that the Iraqi officer's deal with the South Africans could be more on the economic aspect while the deal with Yemen may be something with military considerations.

The conclusion thus became inescapable! Military hardware would have to be dropped in Yemen while the freight of value, treasures and all, would proceed to South Africa. Qassif had brilliantly planned his caper.

Villar's realization strengthened his resolve to fully implement his plan. The hazard of Qassif's designs was great as far as it would affect world peace. If Yemen would accommodate Iraq in its territory where Qassif's compatriots could build a war arsenal and eventually make use of the ally country as a staging ground for attacks on the antagonist forces in the Gulf region, the consequences could be catastrophic not only for the Middle East but for the entire global community as well. Saudi Arabia then becomes a *bibingka*, his favorite native cake back home cooked between two fires. *The madman had to be stopped*!

Villar's hand groped for the grenade in his pocket. It was offered for sale to him by a soldier during one of their stops while edging along the Panama Canal a few days before the US inroad on the Republic of Panama to get General Manuel Noriega. Although he did not find usage for such lethal material then, just the same he made the purchase. Now, he saw its usefulness.

The ship's master wondered whether the Iraqi major's actions had the blessings of his government. He entertained the idea that Qassif may be acting on his own and that his plans did not have the sanctions of Baghdad. Whatever may be the case, Captain Villar made an assurance to himself—Major Qassif would find out too late that, on board *M/V Hope*, all the things he did he had to regret.

"We're listing a bit on starboard," the captain told

the officer-on-watch and the Tunisian. "I think I have to see for myself the cargo stowage in that part of the ship. It may affect our stability once we get out to the ocean."

"Shall I accompany you, sir?" the Tunisian deck cadet inquired, as if suggesting the recourse.

"Come."

The captain, accompanied by the Tunisian, went out of the bridge and proceeded down to the lower portion of the deck. Villar understood. The major may have instructed the Tunisian to keep a close watch on his moves around the ship. Qassif had no trust in him, especially when his actions pertained to the load of the ship.

Villar nodded to the Tunisian as they approached the spot where the heaviest of cargoes were laden. He offered a smile to him which the latter acknowledged with a sheepish grin. *Poor guy. A talent wet to waste.*

The portion of the ship they examined was stacked with crates upon crates of unknown contents which the captain believed to be Major Qassif's war materiel. He supposed these were the cargoes he intended to unload in the port of Yemen.

In all those years of experience on board ocean-going vessels, the captain had developed a thorough familiarization of cargoes transported from one side of the globe to the other. He could almost sense what they were once loaded in his ship. Qassif's crates were unmistakably highly combustible, explosive materials which could turn the vessel into a floating ball of fire through minimum ignition.

Captain Villar lamented the fate of his ship. It did not only lose its name, it had been converted into a strange combination of treasure and firetrap sailing along an eerie sea. Somehow it needed one last redeeming factor.

"Look at how the stowage is done in this portion of the ship," the captain told Alan's successor. The latter sought for a meaning in the captain's statement through the assemblage of crates before him but could find none.

Villar took advantage of the seaman's momentary immobility. He leaned to his right and reached for his boots, then lunged at Alan's successor who was totally puzzled by the situation he was brought into. The suddenness of the assault upon his being appalled the seaman who never expected it. He instantaneously dropped dead on the floor.

The captain threw his bloodstained knife beside the fallen body of the guy who took over Alan's job. His right hand dipped into the pocket of his jacket and took out the grenade. He immediately removed the pin and lobbed it to the pile of crates in front of him.

What ensued was an explosion of great magnitude. Major Qassif was jolted from his sleep. He leaped off his bunk and staggered, rushing out of the owner's cabin. Before his horrified eyes was an unexplained pandemonium which had gripped the ship. No one entertained his queries at the top of his voice. He saw some of his men jumping into the sea.

It was all too sudden and did not take long. The sea was ready to swallow the flaming ship. In a matter of minutes, Major Qassif saw his most precious possession disintegrating.

And so was his own self.

***

"It's gone!"

"What?" Ensign Eaglewood whose consciousness was fleeting came back to full vigilance. His reaction to Brent Brundy's excited voice was automatic. The two of them had become enmeshed in the watch over the vessel which had departed the port of Kuwait. Brundy was almost ready to turn over the screen observation to a reliever but stayed on a little longer upon the prodding of Eaglewood. The former had minimal rest as his eyes were glued to a pair of screens since they plotted the controversial image, being replaced by his reliever only occasionally. To the ensign, Brundy was the most untiring guy on board the *USS Alaska*.

"It simply disappeared from the screen," the navy technician declared.

"What does the *Capricorn* have to say about it?" the ensign asked.

The *Capricorn* represented America's secret, technologically superior war communications system. It consisted of intricate coordinating channels and transmission facilities relying on ultra-sensitive perspective originators augmented by efficient relay programs which the laser-availing components transformed into vivid video flashes with computer precision at its finest. The monitors, too, displayed images at their sharpest. The accuracy of the message imparted was believed to be beyond doubt and the data formation was conceded to be foolproof. The system could also connect with satellite functions.

"Hmnn, tsk, tsk," Brundy merely gesticulated.

"Well…?"

"Probability: the ship exploded, then sank," the navy technician quoted his complex electronic source.

Ensign Eaglewood moved his eyes away, let his thoughts tarry for a moment and turned back to Brundy.

He was almost whispering. "Expunge all data on this matter from the records. Reprogram to the status of events prior to our tracking of that ship."

"Sir?"

"The VRECS has no concern on what had transpired."

Brundy looked up to the ensign for further clarification.

"A report on such sighting of ours wouldn't be for the best interest of world peace," Dean S. Eaglewood continued. "Besides, what happened to that ship has no bearing to our operations in this part of the world."

"But the loss of that ship will be a fact. It is universally known that such ship was docked in Kuwait when the August 2 incident broke out," Brundy expressed concern.

The ensign merely smiled. "The owners of that vessel can always treat the Gulf waters as another Bermuda triangle," he said. "Come to think of it, there's a lot of rest we need to catch up on."

Part 4:
Turnovers

Chapter Fourteen

It was a duplex where Tina stayed with her son Baby Al in one of the suburban areas in the metropolitan capital of the Philippines. She occupied one unit of the same consisting of two bedrooms in the upper floor and a living and dining area in the ground floor. The same set-up in the other unit was maintained by their maternal aunt, a widow who had a daughter schooling as a freshmen in college. The latter assumed the role of baby sitter for Tina's son whenever requested.

The duplex was actually an ancestral house which inured as inheritance of Tina's and Tanya's mother as well as of their aunt from their ascendants. Tina and Tanya were two sisters and so were their mother and aunt. Tina and Tanya had each a room in their unit while their aunt and cousin had theirs in the other. When Tanya went abroad, her room became a chamber for Baby Al's play lessons.

In the morning of the ninth of August, Tina and her cousin were playing with Baby Al when the phone rang. It was Tina's cousin who answered it being nearer to the phone stand.

"Yes, she's here … Tina, it's for you."

"Thanks, Karen."

Tina placed Baby Al on her cousin's lap and took the phone.

"Yes ... Oh, it's you, Dennis, what's the ..."

"Tina, there's news we've received ..."

"What is it, Dennis?"

"There's information received by the shipping company that the crew of *M/V Hope* is now in Amman, Jordan. The Philippine Embassy there confirms that they've already been repatriated from Baghdad."

"How's Alan?" Tina was in high spirits when she came out with the question.

"I'm sorry, Tina, Alan is not one of them," the melancholic tone of Dennis' voice doused cold water on Tina's excitement.

She walked slowly to the crib after putting back the phone, took Baby Al to her arms and whined. "Alan ..."

"Are you all right, Tina?" Karen asked which Tina did not seem to hear.

***

"I think this is a madhouse," Arthur Ng threw a comment to his seated companions who were quite demonstrative of their being exultant as they relished their surprising survival from captivity in a camp in Baghdad. They were now awaiting their flight for Manila, their ETD being in the late afternoon of the day.

"Whatever it is I'd take it, as long I'm assured of home beyond it," an engineer commented.

The quartermaster was among the members of the seamen's group at Jordan's international airport in

Amman who were not able to position themselves in seats for waiting passengers, having run out of available slots. Although the confusion exacerbated the anxiety of those expecting their flights, it was unique on the part of the released hostages as, aside from their newly earned freedom, their repatriation was at hand.

"Who's that guy the chief mate is meeting with?" the QM asked the third mate when he spotted their chief officer approaching four men and a female companion who had just arrived at the airport. An employee from the embassy who had earlier processed their papers facilitated their introduction to each other.

"Don't you recognize him? He's the Philippine Coordinator."

"I've heard a lot about him but never met his person before. By the way, who's that girl with them?" Arthur found out too late that no one was paying him attention. All the eyes of his companions were focused on Tanya.

"She has a facial similarity with Alan's girlfriend," Ben Gomez commented.

"Have you seen her actually?"

"Alan showed me her picture several times, but then ..."

"But then, what?"

"She appears to be—kind of reclusive, appearing to withdraw when a man passes by her."

A woman who was apparently the Coordinator's contact at the airport was seen holding Tanya by the arm and leading her away from men, intending to shun conversation with them.

"Is she a convent girl?" Arthur asked Ben. The latter pretended not having heard him.

Hours later they were aboard a plane soaring through the eastern skies.

***

It was their third afternoon together in the desert and both Myra and Derik realized that the climate was at its finest when compared to the two previous days. The sun had not been too harsh the entire day. In contrast to the lachrymose initial evening that they shared, today appeared to be just as consoling as the second day which, however, was shorter in duration as it took Myra too long to leave the tent where Doctor Khamadi held clinic. She and Grace had volunteered to assist the physician in some of his medical endeavors while Edna stayed with the nanny to keep a constant eye on her although the latter had recuperated fast.

"Let's go a little bit farther," Derik suggested to Myra.

"I'm afraid…."

"Of scorpions?"

"Not anymore. You said they're not coming now that you're here."

"What then are you afraid of?"

"I don't know…."

Derik pointed to a somewhat well-defined spot. "Let's sit there."

Myra turned her head back first before taking Derik's suggestion. "Aren't we far enough? The tents are hardly visible."

"They'll radiate once the lights are on."

"Okay." Myra positioned herself on a portion of the desert chosen by Derik.

When they had settled, awkwardly though it seemed, resting on the sand, Derik repeated a question after laying a jacket on the ground to serve as Myra's cushion.

"Myra, you mentioned you're afraid but unsure of what. You still do?"

"It seems an inherent fear I'm keeping within me. And not only that, I'm worried too."

"Who wouldn't be in this situation?"

Myra held Derik's arm nearest to her in order to emphasize a question. She was seated to his right.

"Why did they let us settle here? How long shall our stay be?

"Don't you notice? We're in the midst of nowhere. If nobody plucks us from here, this could be our permanent living place."

"Oh, no…!" Myra was on the verge of shedding tears again. "When will Peter take me out of here?"

"I'm not a pessimist, Myra, but are you sure the two of you will ever meet again?"

"What do you mean?"

"Could you be so sure Peter got back to that ship, given the hazard which entailed returning to it? If he did, under what condition did the ship sail in troubled waters? And with us here—you think it's possible to get back to the normal world?"

Myra responded to Derik, not with words but sobs.

"Myra, let's accept our fate, whatever it may be," and Derik drew Myra closer to him.

"No, Derik …" Myra intoned a futile refusal. She fell into his both arms and he pressed her closer to his chest.

"Think about it, Myra, despite our separation in a most unusual way, we've been drawn back to each other. It's destiny that is saying it's us."

Then he kissed her cheeks to drive away the traces of tears, and their lips met.

"I'm here, Myra, whatever fortune will come upon us. I'm the one who can respond to your needs now, no other …"

"Derik, please…." Myra felt her sense of longing was being sated by Derik's embrace. She likened herself to an ice melting in the warmth of his kisses.

Myra was not sure what it was that wearied her down—whether the burdensome thought brought about by the dilemma which bugged them or the affectionate hug and the fervent caress she got from Derik. She let her back fall against the covered sand, the heat of which had dissipated, as if in utter helplessness. Derik went on with the kiss, his lips groping for the contour of her body, at the same time shoving her apparel, as the haze overhead grew. Their silhouette which was a merger of two shadows became convoluted as the echoes of passion rose until hush prevailed. Darkness had taken over when they got up, wiping with their hands the grains of sand away from their bodies and shaking off their garments.

They were guided by the illumination from the tents and as they trudged slowly back to the encampment, Derik placed his left arm around Myra's shoulder and at the same time whispering to her the words he long wanted her to have harkened.

"I want to marry you, Myra," Derik said.

***

Alan was quite certain that he had now become comfortable with the Kalashnikov. Clasping the rifle steadily, he began to lower the barrel of his firearm and aimed it towards the street intersection which was empty at the time. He was confident the position of the rifle was steadfast—as firm as his convictions, as sturdy as his heart.

"I think it's already late. Do you believe they're still coming?" Peter who was directly behind Alan asked their two Kuwaiti companions crouched at their side as they waited for the target to come into view.

"They pass this area every night. They will come," said the Kuwaiti.

"So, we'll have to wait some more."

Not long after, the Kuwaiti police patrol car which the Iraqis had commandeered sprang up. Before it was able to turn at the intersection, Alan fired. He hit the front wheels. Peter and their two companions also fired their guns but missed the patrol car which swerved to an embankment beside the road.

It was Peter who fired and hit the driver. The three passengers were, however, quick to disembark and return fire.

"Run!" Alan said to his companions. "They have tremendous firepower. It's overwhelming. Just too heavy for us!"

Alan's group lost no time in so doing. The four of them recoiled in the dark and their shadows instantly melted as the night obscured them. The three Iraqi soldiers carried out a pursuit leaving behind their driver who lolled dead in the front seat of the patrol car.

With all the speed that they could muster, the four resistance fighters were gasping when they reached a portion of the city which was already near their hideout.

"They're gone ... missed us halfway through...." Alan groaned as he tried to regain his normal breathing.

Chapter Fifteen

About the same hour on the day after Tina picked up a call from Dennis to receive the bad news, she was in the same situation with her Baby Al when the phone rang again. It was no longer her cousin Karen who was with her but Dennis himself, coddling her son when the ringing occurred. When she answered it, the unexpected came out to her ear.

"Tanya?"

Dennis, who had his full attention to Baby Al, sat erect and looked straight at Tina exhibiting an utter surprise. He was on leave from work on the tenth of August and paid a visit to his friend's fiancée and their son in the morning of that day. The phone conversation which ensued between the two sisters baffled him.

When Tina put down the phone, she turned frantic and could not make up her mind on how to prioritize her moves.

"Just relax … what did she say?" Dennis attempted to abate her being enkindled.

"She's there. I … we've to see her now."

"Where?"

"The Coordinator's office."

***

Myra had just gone out of a tent with Dr. Khamadi and four other medical workers and volunteers helping out the physician with his patients when an emissary accosted them.

"Doctor, some Iraqi soldiers are visiting you," said the man whom a squad of uniformed men had first run into in the tent city.

When the doctor turned his eyes to the direction the man pointed at, he saw the soldiers approaching.

"Good day! I'm Lieutenant Al Ashadi from the Iraqi Oversight Forces High Command," the leader of the squad introduced himself to the physician. "We've brought nutrients for the refugees."

"Oh, thank you, thank you!" the doctor was profuse with his gratitude as he and the lieutenant reached for each other's hand to come up with a handshake.

Al Ashadi looked around until his eyes caught Myra. She avoided his looks and immediately excused herself from the doctor.

"Thanks, Myra," and the doctor turned his attention to the soldier again.

***

When Tina and Dennis, with the latter carrying Baby Al in his arms, arrived in front of the building housing the MECO, the vicinity was bustling with people. They were relatives of thousands of Filipino contract workers trapped in Iraq and Kuwait. The contract workers' kin stirred Rustico Casabuena's office with queries regarding the plight of their loved ones in the tumultuous countries.

A uniformed male guard met Tina and Dennis at the entrance of the building and two other male employees joined them to ensure that their being led to the Coordinator's chambers was without delay. When the sisters saw each other, they almost jumped and rushed to a tight embrace. Baby Al in the arms of Dennis was crying loudly. The sisters likewise wept as more stories of anxiety unfurled and the sources for grieving unearthed.

The emotional scene led to a more serious conversation until it became clear that three of the vessel's complement were missing. The Coordinator had told them that the seamen on board *M/V Hope* had been repatriated and were with them on the plane from Amman, except the captain who remained with the ship and the two other sailors who were missing—one of whom was Alan. The ship itself had become an object of apprehension among diplomats and shipping officials.

"Whatever happened to Alan ... Where could he be now...?" Tina started to cry as Tanya continued to embrace her.

An uneasy silence prevailed and was broken only by the Coordinator's assuring pronouncement.

"Tanya, your sister and you will be in each other's care now. Your insurance benefits and cash assistance will be immediately processed and should be ready for claiming in a couple of days."

"Thank you, sir."

Soon they all got out of the Coordinator's chambers. The lady guard who in previous days saw the difficulty encountered by Tina in the office was now amazed at the turn of events as the latter and her companions were being guided by the Coordinator himself.

"My car will take you home," he said.

***

It was getting late in the afternoon and Myra was preparing herself to meet with Derik again. She was intrigued, though thrilled, by his proposal of marriage to her. She thought she needed more words from him.

"Myra!"

It was Grace who called out for her. The maid from Kuwait was spending more time with Dr. Khamadi in their charity work and she wondered what it was that brought a certain urgency in the caller's voice.

"What is it, Grace?" she asked.

"The doctor wants you immediately in the medic's tent."

Myra wondered what it was all about. She obliged and hurried to the tent. When she entered, she was shocked to find out no medical personnel was around, except a stranger who was seated on a chair. It was the Iraqi lieutenant she saw earlier in the day.

"Sit down," he signaled Myra towards a stool in front of him.

Myra slowly took a seat, her breath slowly becoming difficult to catch with. "I thought you've left this morning," she finally was able to utter.

"I'm back—with more nutrients."

Silence then took over. But Myra saw the lieutenant intently looking at her.

"Any thing, else ..."

No word was uttered by Al Ashadi in response. Instead, he inserted his left hand in his pocket and took out something. Myra almost collapsed in dismay when she saw what it was—a necklace with a pendant.

"You're the girl in this pendant, aren't you?" he asked.

"I ... no..."

"I'm taking you to Baghdad."

"Nooo!"

At this juncture, two of the lieutenant's men came in and took Myra by her arms.

As they were getting out of the tent, Derik arrived and hollered at the soldiers. "Hey, what are you doing? That's my wife! Where are you taking her?"

"Your wife?" The lieutenant was puzzled.

"Get your hands off me!" Myra was shrieking as she struggled to extricate herself from the soldiers' grip.

"Is that your husband?" Al Ashadi asked, frowning and doubting.

"Yes."

"Well, in that case, you have to do away with him. The colonel wouldn't find a friend in him," the lieutenant ordered his men.

Two of Al Ashadi's men took turns in manhandling Derik until he fell to ground and writhed in pain.

"No...!" Myra was screaming as they dragged her to the car leaving Derik behind.

***

Daylight was gone and Dennis prepared himself to leave. He and the two sisters could not detach themselves from radio and television waiting for every news detail on anything from the Middle East, particularly Kuwait and Iraq.

"What do you think, Dennis?" Tina asked, while Tanya was in shifting attention—glued to TV and at the same time watching over Baby Al whom she had placed on her lap.

"Like what the news has been telling us, Iraq has sealed Kuwait's border…."

"What does that mean?"

"All those in Kuwait who don't have a legitimate reason to stay are in grave peril…!"

***

"Run!"

Alan and his two Kuwaiti companions had to scurry in the usual fashion after having come up with a score. Peter was not with them tonight as he had to be in the company of another group pursuant to an instruction given by The First. This time they were not sure whether they had inflicted a fatal hit. The target was still too far when they did the firing.

"Our strikes are not getting any better. We have more runs than hits," Alan said. His two companions merely nodded.

When they reached the doorstep of their safe-house, Alan made the familiar knocks. In a jiffy he waited and there was none. It was after a few more knocks when the response came and the door suddenly swung open.

It was the barrel of a gun which welcomed Alan. Its nozzle was poked on his chin. The apprentice mate grew pale as more guns were aimed at him and his two companions. A hand grabbed him and pulled his body inside the house. He was stupefied as he saw the faces of the Iraqi soldiers.

It was the end of him!

Three dead bodies were sprawling on the floor. The three resistance fighters bore gunshot wounds in various parts of their limbs. Second Mate Peter Singh was seated on a stool, his hand and feet tied with a rope, while one last remaining alive Kuwaiti resistance fighter, tied like him, sat on the floor.

"Sir Pete, what happened?!"

"They found us, Alan. The others have escaped but these three were unlucky. The two of us were overpowered. We gave up."

The soldiers tied Alan and his companions with a rope, too.

***

It was still dark when the helicopter which brought Myra to an unknown destination landed upon a helipad in the center of a compound surrounded by elegant edifices resembling castles of the medieval era. Myra was astounded by the fast turnover of events that left her addlebrained. Upon being snatched from the village of the tents, she was brought by her captors to a waiting car which negotiated a narrow road to the main highway. At the junction, she was made to board a waiting chopper which whizzed into the blackening sky and finally delivered her to this strange venue.

"To where have you brought me?" Myra asked Lieutenant Al Ashadi as soon as they had disembarked the helicopter.

"This is the headquarters of the Oversight Forces High Command."

Myra looked around but she could hardly obtain a complete perspective of the compound as some portions of it were dark even though certain parts of the buildings were illumined.

"What are you going to do with me here?" Myra again questioned the Iraqi lieutenant.

"You will be subjected to processing."

***

After his hands were tied with a rope, the soldiers blindfolded Alan, too, and brought him to a truck to be transported to a destination he did not know where.

"Sir, Pete?" Alan called out loud.

"I'm here, Alan, they also covered my eyes! I can't see you…."

"Where are the others?"

"I don't know…."

Their conversation was drowned by the roaring of the truck's engine. After less than an hour of traveling, the truck stopped and they were made to step down. The soldiers removed the black cloth covering Alan's eyes and he saw the same thing happening to Peter.

"It's useless covering our eyes. It's night anyway and we couldn't see much of the surroundings," Peter complained to the soldiers.

"Just making sure," the leader said. "Some spots are brightly lighted."

Alan noticed that he and Peter were being moved to a more convenient bus, though smaller, and there were only the two of them in the company of the soldiers.

"Where are you taking us? Where are the others?" he asked.

"They're being treated separately. Since you're of different nationality, summary execution does not apply to you," said the leader of the Iraqi soldiers.

"What is applicable to us?" it was Peter who asked.

"You'll be taken to Baghdad. That's what the rules of the Oversight Forces High Command require us to do."

"Why? What's going to happen to us there?"

"You will be subjected to processing."

Chapter Sixteen

The bus taking Alan and Peter to Baghdad cut across the Iraqi territories with maximum speed and the two seamen mistook the vehicle they were riding on as an airplane streaking through the clouds. The wearisome undertaking they had pursued drained them—both in body and mind—and drove them to somnolence. Their Iraqi escorts were in the same predicament and lost consciousness like they did. Only the bus driver remained vigilant and he exerted every effort to maneuver the bus into attaining the highest velocity with which it was capacitated.

When the bus reduced speed, the two seamen woke up to find that the light of day had taken over. They had gone deep in slumber that they thought they had been drugged into it.

"Where are we?" Alan asked. He was still feeling dizzy as the glaring sunlight struck his already painful eyes and it was as if the prick went to his very heart.

"You're in the camp of the processors," an Iraqi soldier replied.

The two captured seamen looked around the army camp no longer used by the troopers as they were led by their captors to the barracks which would serve as their provisional quarters until their 'processing' would be over. They had no idea where their Kuwaiti colleagues in the resistance movement were nor what had happened to them. They were certain, however, that the natives of the invaded land were due for execution—summarily, that is, if the words of their captors were to be analyzed.

"Filipino seamen were housed here before," the camp attendant who received them commented.

"Filipino seamen?" Alan and Peter uttered in unison.

"Yes. Those taken from a ship docked in Kuwait."

Alan and Peter looked at each other, speechless.

"Where are they now?" Peter intoned after having overcome his puzzlement.

"They've been released."

"Released?" As if unbelieving, Alan sought confirmation.

"Yes. Maybe, they're now in their country of origin this eleventh day of August."

***

Myra was awakened. She had slept in captivity after her arrival in the mesmerizing structure—minutes as soon as she had been thrown into a cell by the soldiers who had brought her therein—due to fatigue and exhaustion, plus the fear. Perhaps this could be the object of such fear she had been complaining about and relayed to Derik in their moments of facing the desert.

The door leading to her cell swung open and a lady soldier together with a man in waiter's attire entered. The latter was bearing a tray with plates full of food and a glass of drink. He placed it gently on a small table beside Myra's bed as a ceiling fan continued to whir overhead to compliment the ventilation of what appeared to be her small pad complete with a comfort room to serve as her temporary abode.

"Enjoy the meal and you'll have more of the amenities later as you are being prepared to meet the colonel," the lady soldier told Myra. "By the way, I am Captain Ehnah, one of his aides."

When she was through with the meal, Myra realized it was past noon already. How time had flown so fast and how the circumstances erupted like bubbles leaving but a single speck of uncertainty— the situation she was now in.

The waiter came back and fixed the mess. Not long after the clearing of her cell, Captain Ehnah arrived and motioned her to get out of it.

"Follow me," the lady captain ordered Myra as they ambled through the hall and took a turn to the stairway leading to the upper floor of the edifice. A few more steps and they stopped in front of one of the doors leading to the rooms situated in that wing of the building.

"Let's get inside," Ehnah invited Myra, having unlocked the door with a key she had brought with her.

Once inside, Myra was awed to note that the room was akin to the best ones they had at the *QRH*. It had an elegant furnishing and the cabinet was replete with a woman's choices for habiliment. Beside it was a door leading to the bathroom.

"Undress your self," a command from the lady captain surprised Myra.

"Huh?"

"You heard me. You've to be clean in person before facing the colonel."

Myra slowly complied.

"All the way," Ehnah stressed on seeing that Myra was clinging to some hesitation. The lady captain entered the bathroom, opened the faucet to infuse water into the bathtub and saw to it that all female accessories were complete.

"Why the ..."

Myra lost track of what she was supposed to say upon seeing Ehnah who likewise undressed herself completely. The lady captain held her by the hand and led her to the bathtub.

"Madam Captain ... what are you up to?" Myra was finally able to mince out the words.

"Like I've said before, you have to be clean thoroughly before you face the colonel."

"But do you have to be on that ... too?"

"It's my job to assure him of the neatness he expects of you. How else could I do it if I'm in full uniform?"

Myra was dazed at what was going on at that very moment. The lady captain held her shoulders and pushed her gently down to submerge her body in the tub which had been filled with water. Then, Ehnah poured body-wash lotion upon her palm, her both feet stepping into the tub to join Myra there. She rubbed the lotion to Myra's neck and nape using both hands, moving down to her shoulders and stopped right before reaching her belly.

"What are you doing?" Myra intoned.

"I have to be sure of your cleanliness," Ehnah replied moving her hands down through Myra's side until she reached her feet. Her left hand moved back upwards.

"That's enough!" Myra yelled with an angry voice as she felt she was shivering—due to the coldness of the water or some strange sensation.

"Okay, okay ... we'll have some shampooing," the lady captain condescended.

When it was over she got a towel and wrapped it around Myra's body.

"You're lucky!" the lady soldier said to Myra.

"Pardon?"

"The colonel opts to marry you even though the two of you haven't met personally, that's why we're into this rigmarole."

"What are you talking about?"

"He'll be taking you as his fourth wife."

"Uh?!"

"The brute has used me several times and yet never proposed marriage to me even for once."

Myra stared at the lady captain and noticed only now that beyond the discomfiting uniform, she was a pretty woman—a beauty to behold especially when she revealed her pulchritude earlier as she bathed with her in the tub. *Only that something failed to fit.*

Ehnah was good at dressing her up, too. Myra was contented at the way she made over her face and entire body. They came out of the room with her as a fashion model.

"You love women, don't you?" Myra asked the captain.

"I do. I like them more than men. With them, it's only ecstasy. With men, it's both ecstasy and pain."

Myra considered the words intriguing. Her mind wandered and searched for analogies. It consequently struck her as befuddling how men had encroached upon her own life—having it with Peter and then Derik. And as she mulled over the affairs, she found it more painful with Derik than with Peter.

And now, he was having this colonel who would take her soon as his wife—the fourth in a row—without both of them having met each other yet! *What a confluence of events beyond belief!*

When they reached the colonel's office, Captain Ehnah knocked twice on the door and without waiting for a response turned the knob.

"Go straight to his visitor's lounge. Colonel Ahfed is expecting you. I already told him who you are and what he'll be expecting from you."

As soon as Myra had gone beyond the door, the lady captain pulled the knob back without peeping inside and walked to the stairway, slowly descending to the ground floor.

Myra's gait was infrequent and her poise awkward as she tramped toward the colonel's lounge where the latter was already seated in a sofa.

"Come, make your self comfortable," the colonel, by way of invitation, motioned Myra to take the separate couch directly facing him in his visitor's lounge.

"Colonel Ahfed ... sir?"

Myra sought confirmation as she confronted a handsome man in his late 30's clad in a colonel's uniform. How he attained that rank at such a young age puzzled Myra and she surmised only one thing could have made it possible—he must be so close to Saddam Hussein to attain it.

"You're prettier in person," he told Myra, with eyes penetrating her physique.

"Sir, pity me … please. I'm just an ordinary girl."

"You're not … from this moment on. In my hands, Myra, you'll be very special," the colonel said as he took out something from his pocket.

Myra saw what it was—her necklace, the pendant of which contained her picture.

"By the way, my dear, will you please tell me how you had my favorite lieutenant killed in that apartment at dawn of August 3?"

Myra was stunned. "Sir? No, I didn't …"

"And how you had my elite squad wiped out in that *QRH*, which initials this pendant of yours bear?"

"No, sir, no!"

"Ha-ha-ha-ha!" The colonel came up with a guffaw which to Myra was frightening.

"Sir, I beg your mercy…."

"Myra, my dear, only a sweet punishment can efface your crime and that is marriage with me," and the colonel went on laughing.

"But you've got enough beautiful women—even if you didn't propose marriage to them."

"Whaat…?! That impertinent gossipmonger!"

Myra saw how the face of the colonel transformed from being an aura of exultation to the ruddiness of rage. He shouted at the top of his voice.

"Bring Ehnah in!"

The colonel's aides scurried and several minutes later they came rushing in to his chambers, the lady captain with them.

"What did you tell the girl?"

"No, sir, please, I didn't tell her anything," Ehnah pleaded.

"Liar!" Ahfed thundered as he pulled out a pistol from his waist and, without much ado, shot the lady captain who dropped on the floor—breathless.

All those in the colonel's chambers froze.

"Take her away," Ahfed ordered his aides.

Myra tried to hold on to herself as she thought she would pass out. After having caught up with her breath, she wiped away the tears rolling down her face which she came to be aware of only when the mess caused by Ehnah's falling down had been settled.

"Myra, you've just seen how I deal with people who lie to me."

Myra thought she was going to faint but the words which Colonel Ahfed subsequently released had enlivened her.

"Don't worry, Myra, it's not going to happen to you."

More words could have come from the colonel but an aide suddenly entered and whispered something to him.

"Alright, bring him in," he told the aide.

In a moment, somebody else came in.

"Oh, Captain Ukuf, my trusted camp commander, you're here. Meet Myra," Ahfed made the introduction which Ukuf acknowledged just slightly as the latter whispered something to the colonel.

"Bring them in, too. Myra would be glad to see her compatriots here."

Chapter Seventeen

Alan was restless as he waited outside Colonel Ahfed's chamber. His eyes were moving around, as if looking for clues as to what he should expect once inside. Peter, on the other hand was immobile, his eyes fixed to the ceiling as he pondered on where all these would lead them to.

Earlier at the camp, Alan fell down on a cot and slouched in frustration after hearing the revelation of the camp attendant—that his fellow seamen from *M/V Hope* had been released and sent home to the Philippines. Must he regret his decision of splitting from them after disembarkation from the ship and when they were being made to board a vehicle which, unknown to him, would ultimately become their conveyance to freedom?

He could not fathom the depth of his remorse and was compelled to raise a question to the second mate.

"Sir Pete, is this really the end of us?" Alan's voice was garbled. The glaring rays of the sun had struck his strained eyes and the prick remained in his heart.

"I guess it is, Alan." The second mate was without qualms; his face was the epitome of a man who had come to learn how to accept one's fate. "Anyhow, all things must come to an end one way or another when their designated time comes. Ours may just be now. We are but prisoners of this world. The choices are not ours."

Peter's words had sealed the lips of Alan. There was nothing else the latter could add nor was he in the position to supplement the second mate's view. Alan, however, entertained the idea that one could not foreclose the coming of a single chance which may yet provide for a leeway.

And now, as they were getting ready to be brought to the colonel, Alan deemed themselves beguiling in their camouflage shirts which the camp attendant issued them, saying: "This will establish your stature as warriors on the opposite side. Besides, the colonel hates talking to unkempt people. He will have the final say on how you shall be treated."

Alan's reverie was interrupted when the door of the chambers gave way.

"The colonel is ready to receive you," a guard called as soon as he emerged from the door.

Peter stepped in first, followed by Alan. As soon as the scene inside the chamber was unfolded before their eyes, shock overwhelmed the two seamen. Myra, too, was flustered, her eyes glowing as she coped with the unexpected.

"Peter...?"

"Myra...?"

The two were startled by the incredulity of the situation inside Colonel Ahfed's chambers. They were at a loss on how to react to the state of things now fully unraveled before their senses, brushing aside the impression that this was just a joke or a mere dream. There could not be a denial of reality. On the part of Alan, he stood erect and remained speechless—being dumbfounded.

"How did you get into this … Myra?"

"Peter, weren't you aboard the ship? Why…? The two of you—how did all these reach the present stage?"

Peter wanted to run toward Myra and embrace her and the latter moved to rise up and welcome him, but the Iraqis prevented them from doing so. The guards held Peter's arms tightly while Myra's hands were held by the colonel who had suddenly stood up.

"The two of you … close to each other before? Not now. I'm taking her as my wife," the colonel spoke. Although directed primarily to Peter, it was for the absorption of all.

At this juncture, there was a knock on the door and Lieutenant Al Ashadi showed up when it opened. He went straight to the colonel, rendered a salute and, after it was acknowledged, whispered something to him which was not quite inaudible.

"The overseer has arrived, sir. He wants to see you."

"Can't it wait a little while? I'm winding up with this people."

"He says now."

"Okay … Wait a while, I'll be back." And the colonel darted toward the door after addressing all those in his chambers.

Peter took advantage of the situation—he rushed to Myra, brushing aside the grip of his guards who had loosened it when the colonel left. The girl, initially manifesting excitement upon seeing Peter, had gradually mellowed, and when Peter drew near to reach out for her, she raised her hands to stop him. She shunned his eyes, too.

"Myra, what are you up to? Isn't it significant to you that I'm here?"

Myra shook her head and closed her eyes, her tears having fallen.

"Yes, we're in a precarious situation but it doesn't matter. What counts is—I'm here!"

"No, Peter, you don't understand. Things are different now."

Peter inched closer to Myra but this time the guards prevented him.

"Myra, please, be in your right sense … Don't let your emotions consume you…!"

A guard held back the second mate and another pushed him away from Myra who now had wept. Peter deigned and settled in a corner of the chambers with the guards while continuing to focus his eyes on Myra who had stooped as she nursed her wounded feelings.

"Don't disturb her. She's set to marry the colonel," said one of the guards.

It was Peter's turn to moan and let out a sigh—and cry. Alan sported a wry face, sneering and smirking interchangeably like one who had suddenly gone out of his mind.

Inside the overseer's chamber, the latter was seated in his swivel chair, casting a penetrating look at the colonel who saluted him upon entrance but which he did not acknowledge. The man was bemustached and had an imposing face, radiating an aura of conceit that sent scruples to those who may come across him. He did not even motion the colonel to take a seat as he started berating him.

"More than a week had lapsed and you didn't even send a single word to me about that ship!" he snarled at the colonel.

"Sorry, sir, I ... I ..."

"And where's that thief Qassif? Why is he silent as the meekest of lambs?"

"No, sir ..."

"Don't give me no for an answer!"

"Yes, sir."

"You know fully well that there are only the three of us who are privy to this thing."

"I do, sir."

"And you ordered the precipitate release of those we had plucked from the ship without first verifying whether we already obtained our end of the bargain."

"Sorry, sir."

"I want you to produce Qassif before me in twenty-four hours. No ifs and buts!"

"Yes, sir."

When Colonel Ahfed came back to his chambers, it became outright evident to those who had seen him leave his office earlier that there was a total turnaround in his mood, the looks of his face had gone unpleasant and it appeared he lost touch with everybody.

"All of you leave my chamber," he bawled out. "Send the three of them to the camp."

"The lady, too, sir?" Captain Ukuf tried to verify.

"Don't you know how to count? I said three!"

"Yes, sir."

"And you come back tomorrow an hour before the current time."

"Yes, sir!" There seemed to be a chorus for all of those in the colonel's chamber.

A crew cab was waiting in the parking lot of the edifice where the colonel held office. Alan took the front seat with the driver while Peter and Myra occupied the back seat. Their armed three escorts were positioned at the open back section of the vehicle.

Peter held Myra's hands and, although she did not resist, she nevertheless leaned away from him.

"Myra …"

She shut her eyes—as she did not know how to face reality.

The camp attendant brought them to a different area when they reached there. It was actually a cottage behind the one occupied by the camp commander. There were two rooms in it, a small lounging area and lavatory. The pantry was replete with the occupants' needs.

"They really made out real guests in us," Alan observed.

"Ambience before hanging the two of us, maybe?" Peter replied.

"Peter, don't say that!" Myra snapped.

"Excuse me …" Alan immediately left his two companions inside the cottage and went out to sit on the steps before its entrance door. There, he started musing again as the couple inside held on to their drama.

"Why did he relent? He said he was taking you as a bride. Why did he postpone your wedding if indeed one was going to take place? He knows I'm hot on you, and yet, why did he send the two of us here ... together?

"Peter ... I can't figure out anything."

"I find it strange, too."

"And why is my necklace with him?"

Peter looked away for a while trying to piece together the fragments of his thoughts. Then he concluded. "Those soldiers in the apartment—they must be his men."

Peter, standing in front of Myra who was seated on a sofa, stepped forward and sat beside her. He took her hands and found out they were cold. He wrapped her arms around her. She was frigid. He placed his lips on her cheek and moved on to her mouth. This time she squirmed.

"No, Pete ..."

"Why, Myra, why?"

"I've become unworthy of your affection. I've given up myself on us!"

"No, Myra, not even that beast can take you away from me."

And Myra's protestations were drowned by Peter's passionate stance. She felt like a leaf being plucked from a drooping branch swayed by the wind and flown to a desert, the arid sand of which was being drenched by a drizzle. In Myra's fantasy, that night in the desert with Derik flashed, but it was momentary as it simply turned evanescent. Lately did she realize that Peter had carried her in his arms and brought her to one of the two rooms in the cottage. There, the longing they had subdued in their hearts was sated.

When it was over, Myra stood up and gathered her clothing which Peter had hastily removed from her and thrown elsewhere. It was the same clothing which the poor and unlucky Captain Ehnah dressed her up with. Peter admitted that she looked lovely in it.

"You'll be wearing it again tomorrow," Peter uttered with a voice imbued with a complaining tone.

Myra had the garment hung up and she wrapped instead a towel around her body. "Can't do otherwise," she begrudgingly uttered.

As she sat down on the bed beside Peter, her thoughts lingered. Should she reveal to Peter what she went through with Derik? It would not matter anyway. She could not be anyone's woman at all with her impending taking by the colonel.

And she did. The mood in the room turned dreary when she came up with the narration, occasional sobs being eked out by her as Peter's teeth gnashed, his fists clinched—and yet there was nothing he could do against her.

"I was resigned to being marooned in the desert. No one there could provide me a supporting hand but him. And I thought it wasn't possible to ever see you again," Myra said in a dispirited voice.

"And the worst is yet to come," Peter's voice was even more dejected.

In the midst of the plaintive atmosphere which prevailed in the room, Peter and Myra fell into each other's arms once more.

Outside, a faraway scenario preoccupied Alan's mind. He saw Tina and their son clinging to each other, as if in a dream. They were calling him out loud.

***

Indeed, they were.

It was late afternoon in Manila and Tina stood at the door of their residential unit in a duplex house in the suburban portion of the metropolis. She got accustomed to the visits of Dennis Nillos during the early evenings, usually at past six, as there was always news that he would be bringing. Tonight would be no exception. Inside, her sister Tanya was busy, her preoccupation being a baby sitter for Baby Al.

She was cajoling the baby to call for his father. "Call daddy, Baby Al, your daddy's Alan ... Alan, Baby Al's waiting for you...."

Such role Tanya had assumed provided for some sort of a palliative to her, as her mind was diverted from the unpleasant to a caring with satisfaction— aside from providing her sister with the needed assistance while the latter served in dual capacity: both as mother and father to her Baby Al. She hoped something would come to serve as panacea for all the inequities that came into her being.

A little while lapsed and Dennis arrived. He was a little bit late but it was compensated by the nice things he brought: a new rattle for Baby Al and native cakes for the two sisters they were fond of eating. Tanya was particularly excited about those cakes as she had missed them during her period of employment in Kuwait.

"It's fast becoming a mystery—I mean, the fact that until now no news of the ship boarded by Alan has been circulated," Dennis announced to the two sisters.

"I think we should ask the Coordinator tomorrow when I get back to his office," Tanya suggested.

"How come most of its crew are back here on the same flight with the Coordinator, and yet the ship itself is missing—Alan especially?" Tina made known her worries.

"Don't you think Alan jumped ship?" Dennis opined.

"Why would he do it?" Tina expressed.

"He was in high spirits the last time I met him in the hotel," Tanya revealed.

"I suspect a more fearsome consequence."

"Dennis, please, don't send us to panic," the two sisters pleaded.

Chapter Eighteen

The same vehicle which brought them to the camp the day before arrived and stopped right in front of the cottage occupied by Captain Ukuf's 'guests' before three o'clock in the afternoon of the twelfth of August. Myra, Peter and Alan were ready to board the same on the trip back to the colonel's chambers. They were attired in the same outfit they wore when they first met Ahfed. As the vehicle left the camp, its commander rode in his own car and instructed the driver to tail closely the crew cab.

When the door opened and the three captives were ushered in, they found that Colonel Ahfed was not in his chambers. The guards told them to just wait as he would be arriving soon. Myra and Peter positioned themselves in a sofa while Alan took the couch.

Minutes later, an officer arrived but it was not Ahfed—it was Al Ashadi.

"Where's the colonel?" Captain Ukuf, who was closely guarding his 'guests' while seated beside Alan, asked the lieutenant.

"He's at *The Marina* waiting. I am under instructions to take you there and see to it that you arrive safely and in time," Lieutenant Al Ashadi disclosed.

Three vehicles zoomed toward the place which the lieutenant mentioned minutes after he made the announcement. The convoy was led by Al Ashadi's military van. Following it was the vehicle with the three captives on board while Ukuf tailed them in his car.

"Pete … I think this is where my fear becomes real. It's no longer an imagined fear now …" Myra held on to Peter as the vehicle progressed toward their destination.

"Keep your embrace tight, Myra, it's us till the end," Peter drew Myra's head closer to his chest.

Alan heard their voices aching as he struggled to visit again the dream—perhaps, a nightmare—that shook him as the night that passed wore out and gave way to the present day. He saw a hangman swaying his rope. He placed it on his neck and started to tighten the noose. While feeling the pressure around his neck, Alan could no longer hold back the tears flowing down his face—the shedding of which was meant not only for himself and his loved ones but for all others to whom fate had been unkind or to those whose hopes had to be crushed at a cruel crossroad. He knew what was taking place at that precise moment: the end of a beautiful hope and of an idealism fraught with bitterness. When the hangman pulled the rope, his eyes opened—back to reality. But the tears were still there.

"We're here," the driver of the crew cab announced when they reached the place referred to as *The Marina*.

Alan stepped down from the vehicle and he was followed by Peter and Myra. *The Marina* came to his view in full. Situated on an elevated portion along the western bank of the Tigris River, it resembled some resorts commonly advertised by certain countries to promote their tourism programs and could be mistaken as a miniature model of the same. It was surrounded by a wire fence attached to concrete posts atop of which incandescent lamps had been installed while the wide entrance was protected by a gate constructed out of steel bars. They entered the area upon signal from the guards and Alan was able to have a complete sight of the landscaped scenery, in the middle portion of which a swimming pool separated the rock fountainhead from the clubhouse. There was a side gate leading to the concrete steps which descended to a mini-wharf where a yacht and a speedboat were moored.

The colonel came out of the clubhouse upon seeing that they had arrived. He went straight to the point. "Let's start the game. We're running out of time."

Alan, as well as Peter and Myra, became puzzled as they were clueless on what the colonel was up to.

"What's he talking about?" Alan asked his two companions.

"I'm sensing a strange objective on his part," Myra's expression showed that she was beginning to turn more frantic.

Peter said nothing. He was in thorough analysis of the colonel's designs and concluded that something sinister was growing in Ahfed's mind.

Even the colonel's men found it difficult to decipher his words as Ukuf and Al Ashadi looked at each other inquisitively. The lower-ranked troopers who were with them likewise did.

All of a sudden, Ahfed drew out his handgun and aimed at a lamp atop one of the concrete posts where the wire fence was attached. He fired it and the lamp exploded. Then he pointed the firearm to Alan and Peter alternately.

"Go down the steps and take the speedboat. All three of you!" The colonel ordered, looking furious.

They were left without a choice but to comply. And as they began taking the descending steps, the colonel shouted, "Myra!"

The three of them turned their heads up to the colonel while they were halfway through the concrete steps leading to the mini-wharf. Even the colonel's men were curious as their eyes were fixed on him.

Colonel Ahfed took out a necklace from his pocket and threw it to Myra but it was Peter who caught it for her with his right palm. It was the same necklace with the pendant containing her picture therein which was still intact.

"It's all yours, I've no more use for it," Ahfed declared.

The three of them set foot on the mini-wharf and looked back to the colonel who was standing overhead with his men beside him to seek for further instructions.

"Do you know how to handle that thing? It's ready to be operated," Ahfed asked, moving the nozzle of his gun towards the direction of the speedboat.

"Of course!" It was Peter who answered. "I'm an officer of the ship, a full-fledged sailor. It's too small a thing when measured in my capacity."

As Peter prided with himself, Ahfed lowered his pistol. "Good! Occupy the speedboat now."

"Okay!" And the three of them hurriedly boarded the water-borne contrivance.

"Start now! As I aim, it behooves upon you to make sure that my bullet misses you, otherwise it would be the endgame."

And the speedboat buzzed, slicing through the water as the colonel sought precision with his aim.

"Sir Pete, don't follow a straight course. Pursue a zigzagging route to mislead him, so he'll get confused with his target," Alan suggested.

As Peter maneuvered through a crooked course, the colonel's hand likewise shifted directions and could not establish a precise target.

"Shoot now, sir, they're getting far and you're onto a diminishing target," Captain Ukuf advised the colonel.

Ahfed turned to the captain and aimed his pistol at him instead. "Don't tell me what to do and don't you ever doubt my capacity to shoot!"

"No, sir, please!" It was Al Ashadi who pleaded with the colonel as the muzzle of his firearm shifted from the captain's direction to the lieutenant.

And to their dismay, the colonel suddenly placed the tip of his pistol upon his own breast, directly on the spot where his heart was located—and squeezed the trigger. Colonel Ahfed went down like a tree being felled—with a broken heart. *Literally and otherwise.*

The uniformed men could not believe what they were witnessing. They rushed to the colonel whose fallen body was undeniably lifeless when it settled to the ground.

"What's that?" Peter who was relentlessly maneuvering the speedboat yelled upon being aware of the gunshot which, although faint, he could still distinguish.

"Continue with the dash, Sir Pete, they might be shooting at us," Alan yelled back.

It was Myra who turned to where the sound of gunshot came from. *The Marina* had turned to a vanishing sight but the trouble going on there could still be sensed by her.

Meanwhile, as Captain Ukuf and Lieutenant Al Ashadi, with the rest of their men, rushed to where the colonel had collapsed, a truckload of black-attired, gun-wielding men arrived at *The Marina*.

The two officers curiously turned their attention to them. "Who are these guys?" Ukuf inquired from Al Ashadi.

"They're men from Central Command, I suspect," the lieutenant surmised.

The leader of the men in black approached them. He was holding a pistol which he had just removed from his holster.

"What have you done? You preempted us on our mission!"

And without hesitation, he fired his firearm at Ukuf and Al Ashadi. Mayhem followed. A series of sound cracking and bursting perturbed the otherwise placid atmosphere which characterized the surroundings, and when it was over, it resulted to more fallen bodies, wiping out the entire group of Colonel Ahfed.

The men in black went back to their truck and left *The Marina*, taking their own men who had fallen.

"Hurry! Hurry!" It was Myra shouting at Peter as Alan helped him out with the wheel. When she looked back later, *The Marina* could no longer be seen.

"What's this?" Peter asked himself, perplexed.

"What...?" Alan and Myra asked Peter, too, together.

"The speedboat is not responding to my maneuvers anymore. The wheel ceases to function. The speed can't be reduced."

"What shall we do?" Myra expressed worry.

"It will explode if it smashes into something really hard," Peter cautioned.

"We have to abandon this speedboat," Alan suggested.

"We're headed toward a coming boat!" Myra pointed to a watercraft sailing southward along the wide river and coming to their direction.

As the floating steel neared them, they saw that it was a barge and was almost certain to collide with the uncontrollable speedboat carrying them.

"Jump!" Peter shouted.

They acted simultaneously, throwing their bodies overboard. Their speedboat continued to advance swiftly to the direction of the barge and several minutes later slammed on its side causing it to explode. With its sturdy construction, the barge appeared to remain unaffected—or so it seemed.

Later, several crew members of the barge threw them three doughnut-shaped lifesavers which they held on to until the crew members on board were able to pull them out of the water and onto the barge.

"Give them something to change with. They're all wet," the skipper of the barge ordered his men.

As they were being handed their provisional clothing which consisted of the seamen's working outfit, Alan noticed that the barge was carrying uniformed Iraqi soldiers. Myra clung to Peter's arms when she noticed, too.

***

Tanya had finished dressing up Baby Al when Tina called saying she had already contacted a taxi.

"Alright, we're ready, too," and Tanya lifted her nephew, went out of the room and negotiated the stairs to the ground floor of their dwelling unit.

"Where's the taxi?" Tanya asked when she saw that the vehicle was not yet parked in front of their door.

"A matter of minutes and it will be here. I've already requested a pedicab driver to signal one he might meet in the crossing—that there are passengers here waiting."

After Tina spoke, a taxi arrived and Tanya directed the driver to proceed to the MECO. When they arrived there, the Coordinator was not in his office. But before five in the afternoon, Tanya received her checks from the releasing section of the agency.

"Dennis said to me yesterday he'll fetch us here after five," Tina told Tanya.

"Well, we might as well wait for him. This office extends services by hours considering the exigency that it is working on," Tanya replied.

In less than half an hour, Dennis arrived.

***

"Where are you from?" the skipper questioned the three after having disposed of their wet clothes.

Alan and Peter looked at each other. Myra was pale and speechless. It was Alan who found the words for an answer. "We're employed at *The Marina*. Our speedboat malfunctioned."

"*The Marina?* A resort for the Oversight Forces," commented one of the soldiers.

"That reclusive command?" asked another.

"We're soldiers from the Engineering Battalion. We've departed from Baghdad bound for Basra to do some infrastructure work," a sergeant introduced themselves to the three civilians.

"We're happy to be with you here despite our fears due to what happened to our speedboat. By the way, this is my wife, Myra," Peter introduced his girlfriend to the soldiers and the crew.

Myra flashed an uneasy smile for the group. *Whew, several people have claimed me to be wife for them*, Myra mused. *I'm for Peter, of course.*

Many in the group expressed gladness in having met her. Myra touched her necklace and its pendant. She wore it after Peter had passed it on to her, having caught it when Ahfed threw the same.

"People in this barge appear to be good natured," Myra whispered to Peter when the night had progressed. "They seem to treat us like their real guests."

"I saw that, too. A sharp contrast to the behavior of those who come from the Oversight Command," Peter whispered back.

Alan who was seated on the edge of a cot where the two lovers lay found it imperative to share a whisper. "There's something that bugs me."

"What is it, Alan?" Myra tried to verify.

"The colonel may have been smitten by you, Myra."

"What do you mean?"

Alan turned to Peter instead. "Wasn't it because of Myra that our fellow sailors from *M/V Hope* were released, Sir Pete?"

"It occurs in my mind only now, Alan," Peter rose from the cot.

"And do you think Colonel Ahfed was serious in making us his target?"

Peter and Myra were rendered immobile. "Don't you suspect that gunshot from *The Marina* as not being intended for the three of us? That it was meant for another person instead?"

The night grew deeper and it left more questions unanswered.

Chapter Nineteen

"It has gotten off course!"

But no one heard him as his single companion in the room was snoring. Brent Brundy turned his head to his superior, Ensign Dean S. Eaglewood, and studied his profile. He wondered why despite his lean physique the ensign was a noisy snorer; he thought such characteristic belonged only to fat people.

Brundy decided to awaken his boss. "Sir, there's something interesting here."

"You … sure?" Eaglewood rubbed his eyes, got up and went to Brundy's side, bending his body down at the left of his technician to get a glimpse of what was going on in his monitor.

"Hmnn …" the ensign stood erect.

"It has gone astray and drifting toward our area of concern."

"Indeed."

"So …" Brundy was not able to utter more words when he saw that Eaglewood had gone back to his table and picked up his receiver, dialing at the same time.

"The *Dragonfly Ace* leaves immediately," the ensign declared after replacing the receiver.

The *USS Alaska* had pushed farther into the Persian Gulf escorted by two warships from the *New*

York fleet. And inching closer to the crisis area, it aimed to intensify its snooping at the countries involved.

***

At dawn, Alan woke up to a portentous silence. The cot on which Peter and Myra had slept could hardly accommodate the two of them who lay in embrace; thus, Alan had to settle on a remaining space at their feet by slouching therein. After looking around and seeing that some soldiers had begun to become restive, he touched the shoulders of Peter to wake him up as the latter had buried himself in deep slumber wrapped by the comforting arms of Myra.

"What is it, Alan?"

The apprentice mate whispered something to him as Myra woke up too. A sudden surge of vigilance sent the second mate standing up.

"Oh, no, the engine isn't working! We're adrift!"

"Oh …" Myra raised a concern. "Didn't our speedboat cause it?"

No one answered her. The mood on board the barge had grown to frenzy as daylight was unfolding.

"What happened?" a soldier was overheard shouting.

"The engine conked out while it was still dark!" somebody from the pilothouse replied.

It was a clear morning and an hour later everybody on board panicked when they heard the unexpected. "Mine ahead!"

"Abandon ship!" the skipper declared.

Not letting a moment to lapse, the soldiers quickly jumped into the water from the starboard portion of the barge carrying with them whatever they could—lifejackets and lifesavers—to keep them afloat.

Alan, Peter and Myra froze. They realized it was too late to make any move. The soldiers had brought all the lifesaving equipment with them and nothing was left to the three civilians. Myra threw herself at Peter who caught her with a tight embrace. Meanwhile, before the horrified eyes of Alan, an object at sea which caused uproar among the soldiers was getting near as the barge continued to drift toward it.

Alan closed his eyes and began to pray. When he later opened his eyes, sensing that nothing had happened, he realized what it was.

"It wasn't a mine, Sir Pete, but a mere buoy gone wayward."

The lovers heaved a sigh of relief.

"I'm hungry," Myra complained.

"Let's see what the crew had left behind," Alan suggested.

"Proceed to the galley, then," Peter remarked and in an instant they did.

At the galley, they sought for the pantry and found that there were indeed provisions left behind which were enough to cure their hunger.

Hours later, Alan sat trying to disabuse his busy mind with some difficult thinking. Peter who was standing at the starboard side stared at the sea after having let go of Myra who went to the port side and gazed at the firmament.

"What's that?" Myra voiced out upon seeing an object in the sky.

Alan immediately ran and saw it, too. "An aircraft!"

Peter who finally joined them came up with a move. "Let's ascend to the roof deck!"

As the aircraft was nearing them, they saw that it was a helicopter, but not an ordinary one. It was capsule-shaped with somewhat pointed tip, propelled by twin rotors of four airfoil blades each and did not produce an irritating noise. As it approached the space directly above them, a man's head protruded from the side and, holding a megaphone, announced: "We're lowering the rope ladder. Take it immediately one by one."

Peter caught the tip of the rope ladder and immediately assisted Myra to take steps onto it. The chopper's crew pulled it up while their craft whirred in stationary mode. When it was thrown down again, it was Peter's turn to climb. The third lowering of the rope was for Alan but barely had he grasped it when the chopper swayed and soared to farther heights with the crew struggling to pull the seaman up. As soon as Alan made it to the helicopter, the barge exploded and was engulfed by flames.

"Thanks … Thank you very much for saving us," Myra was profuse in expressing her gratitude to the crew of the chopper.

The two sailors likewise expressed their own by reaching out for the hands of those who had saved them.

"Welcome … Welcome aboard the *Dragonfly Ace*," the pilot greeted them. "This is our most modern chopper technology, convertible to warrior's response with jet zooming capacity."

"Your watercraft was drifting to a mined area," one of the men in the helicopter told them. "The mines were placed there during the Iran-Iraq war in the 1980's and there are few still remaining which have not been detonated."

"Where are we headed for?" Peter asked their American host. There was no mistaking about it. He was wearing a jacket adorned by an insignia with stars and stripes in it.

"*USS Alaska*. You'll undergo orientation, briefing and medical examination on board."

***

Tanya and Tina spent the entire afternoon of August thirteenth waiting for news that would address their curiousness but as it turned out nothing had been forthcoming. Tina tuned in alternately to the radio and TV while Tanya leafed through the pages of both broadsheet and tabloid she had gotten hold of.

"Tanya, don't you think I should take Dennis' advice?" Tina asked her sister, interrupting the latter's concentration on the papers.

"About what?"

"That I should take up an employment. There's no more allowance from an ocean-going vessel which Baby Al and I can share with Alan. Besides, we can't rely on your monetary benefits from the MECO and the insurance proceeds. That will be depleted if not replenished."

Tanya put down the papers and looked at her sister intently. "Well ..."

"Dennis said he could help me out as a casual employee in their agency. He's so close to his boss."

"Let's think about it."

Dennis later arrived and this time no native cake was brought by him. Instead, noodles and roasted chicken were unwrapped by him and the sisters got convinced that the time for supper had come, which the three of them should share.

Tina took charge of the mess as Dennis watched TV. Tanya took Baby Al to her room and prepared him for sleep—but it did not come immediately. When the baby boy finally stopped moving and turned silent, Tanya felt that her eyelids became heavy, too, and lost consciousness.

When Tanya recovered from her lethargy, she surmised that more than an hour may have lapsed since she passed out. She rose from the bed she shared with Baby Al and opened the door of her room. Halfway through the stairs leading to the ground floor where the living room was, she saw both Tina and Dennis having gone asleep, too. Tina's head was resting on Dennis' left shoulder. An odd feeling suddenly overwhelmed Tanya. She did not continue with her descent through the stairway and instead went back to her room, lying beside Baby Al again in her bed.

An hour later, she heard the door opening and saw Tina coming in to her room to take her son. She got up and confronted her sister.

"What are you doing, Tina?"

"What do you mean?"

"You seem to have developed a kind of closeness to Dennis that's beyond the normal level."

Tina was silent for a while, then she sat down beside her sister on the latter's bed and wept.

"Dennis said he wants to marry me."

"Whaat?"

"He believes Alan couldn't have made it and I shouldn't wait in vain forever. Besides, I need arms, loving and caring—supportive, too—and shoulders to lean on ... things I've been deprived of since Alan left me before Baby Al was born. That was more than a year ago."

"Is he serious?"

"I agree with him, sister. I've got the same perception. I think he's absolutely right." And Tina fell into Tanya's arms, the latter embracing her and shedding tears, too.

"What kind of feelings do you have for him, Tina?" Tanya asked, wiping away her tears.

"I got a crush on him the first time I saw him during Alan's graduation ball. He and his girl friend were in the same hotel that I and Alan spent the night with. I think he's an admirable guy."

Chapter Twenty

At noon of the day that followed, the results were out and the same were favorable to the three examinees on board the *USS Alaska*. It became an occasion for the three Filipinos to meet persons of consequence on board as well as marvel on the facilities of the modern ship.

"Hi, I'm Brent Brundy," one of those to whom they were introduced revealed his name. "From VRECS."

"VRECS … what is it?" Myra became inquisitive.

Brundy told her about it.

"Oh, it's awesome … but too complicated for me."

Peter, who had intently listened, found an opportunity to butt in. "Me, too."

"Interesting," Alan commented.

"Ah, here's my boss, coming," Brundy became excited when he saw Eaglewood approaching.

"Hi!" the ensign greeted them.

"He's the man who sent you the *Dragonfly Ace*. We've seen you drifting to a hazard zone," Brundy introduced his boss to the three.

"Oh, how grateful we are, sir," Myra expressed her gratitude with a firm handshake while her male counterparts saluted the ensign.

After acknowledging them, Eaglewood made the announcement. "Early tomorrow, you'll join some of our troopers on board our *Flyer One*."

"What's that?" Myra could not help but become excited with every new word she heard.

"One of our personnel carriers which would take you to Diego Garcia."

"What have we got to do there?" It was Alan's turn to ask a question.

"Expect your turnover. George Bush is sending you home," Eaglewood said.

***

"I always had in mind Diego Garcia as a rugged Guantanamo-type venue for American assembly of war materiel, vessels, aircraft and all those lethal machines, but admittedly I am mistaken," Peter commented when they were already resting in Bangkok, Thailand.

"I share you thinking, Sir Pete, and furthermore I had the impression that it's a place to be shunned," Alan expressed his own comment.

"I never heard that place before. When the ensign first told us that we would be brought there, I thought he was turning us over to a certain warlord who's an ally of America. It was only later when I realized he was referring to their military base in the Indian Ocean," said Myra. "To me, it's paradise island converted to a warriors' hub."

They arrived in the island before the fifteenth of August waned and spent the following day basking in the white sand and clear water of the coral atoll, more than fifteen square miles in lateral extent and shaped like a man's sock floating in the middle of the Indian Ocean.

They enjoyed fully the day as if it was the first time in their lives that they had visited a resort island although in their own country there were several beach resorts that could qualify as paradise in the making, yet readily accessible.

They wound up their enjoyment with a revisit to tragedy which to Alan was a shocking revelation. When Peter and Myra disclosed to him what Tanya went through at the ill-fated hotel, based on Derik's narration to Myra when they were in the desert, the apprentice mate wriggled in pain, unable to hold back his tears while clinching his fists. He found it difficult to say a word and had to be left alone for sometime to nurse his smarting sentiment induced by the wretchedness which befell Tanya.

"I know Tanya will get through with it. She's the kind who wouldn't bow to that sort of misfortune. She'll rebuild her life as a chance will come her way to do so," Myra envisioned.

Alan was shaking a bit but nodded at the same time. "My homecoming would have been perfect. Tina and Baby Al are expecting me joyfully and if not for the sadness Tanya brings, everything will boil down to happiness and contentment."

"Don't nurture the sadness in your heart, Alan. For all the inequities, there'll always be a healing," Myra consoled the apprentice mate.

* * *

The Philippine Embassy in Thailand, situated in its capital Bangkok, informed the three Filipino overseas contract workers that they were slated for enplaning to Manila on the twentieth of August after they were turned over by the US authorities from Diego Garcia on the seventeenth. Alan, Peter and Myra could hardly wait for their flight on board the Philippine Airways. They eagerly waited for their scheduled departure late in the afternoon of the designated day.

When the public address system made the announcement, on the day of their departure, that their plane was ready to accept passengers, Myra and Peter immediately rose and positioned themselves after the two men in the queue while Alan lined himself after the three women following the couple. Inside the plane, the apprentice mate was seated at the back of Peter and Myra who were oblivious of the other persons around them as they remained locked in arms and oftentimes whispering to each other. Alan, however, was in deep thought, planning what moves to take upon arrival in Manila.

It was darkness which welcomed them when the plane touched down at the country's premier airport. As they were about to go their separate ways, Alan hugged Peter while Myra inched closer to the former and rendered a cheek-to-cheek farewell bid.

"Cheer up, Alan and keep in touch with us," Myra let out her parting words to the apprentice mate.

Alan proceeded to his uncle's house in the outskirts of Manila as the latter was an accountant in one of the nearby factories and lived with his cousins there, being a widow. His own parents resided in the province, about a hundred kilometers from the metropolis. It was utter surprise which they exhibited when they saw him. Alan spent the night in their house.

The apprentice mate woke up to a morning different from all other days he had previously opened his eyes to. There was no disabling fear, no compulsion, no qualms. The tiredness caused by all that he had been to downed him and the preceding night had sent him to total blackout. Regaining his consciousness and strength, he set out to meet the ensuing sunny day.

There was no hassle which Alan encountered when he located the duplex residence where he used to fetch and visit Tina during the days prior to his boarding the ship as an apprentice mate. With delight and a smile on his face, he knocked on the door which readily opened. It was Tina's cousin who greeted him.

"A nice day, Karen. How's your cousin Tina?" Alan asked the girl.

"Sorry, they're not here. I've been left alone to see about their unit for a day. They'll be coming back tomorrow after spending a day in a resort," Karen answered with a somewhat discouraging voice.

"They left early for a stint in the resort?"

"They'll go to a judge of the metropolitan court first. Tina and Dennis are getting married!"

Alan thought he was hit by a monkey fist on his forehead. If his subsequent grasp of the door knob was not tight, he could have collapsed.

"Oh, my ... Is it a joke, Karen?"

"No. Their marriage ceremony has been set in the metropolitan court this morning." The words coming from Karen were too succinct that they left no room for an interpretation in another way.

Alan lost no time. He immediately scurried from the dwelling unit and chased an empty taxi which had passed by. He was panting when he settled into the seat behind the driver.

"Please hurry. I need to catch up with someone … something in the metropolitan court," Alan pleaded with the driver.

The cab driver obliged, and in a jiffy, his vehicle was cruising along the narrow and winding roads of the city. He guessed it was already past nine when he arrived at the duplex where Tina dwelt. Now, he was racing against time.

When he reached the metropolitan court, he paid the taxi driver the fare without bothering to collect his change. He immediately ran to the door of the court's branch in the ground floor and opened it. To his surprise, there was no marriage ceremony taking place.

Making inquiries, he was able to acquire from one of the court employees a suggestion. "Why don't you visit the branch situated on the third floor?"

"Thanks."

Alan thought he was on an uphill climb as he clambered up through the stairs leading to the third floor. When he opened the door of the courtroom, he saw a judge officiating marriage who seemed disturbed by his arrival.

The man and the woman being wed by him were also affected, turning their heads to find out who it was who came late. Alan saw that the bride was not Tina. Neither was the groom Dennis.

"Sorry … so sorry," Alan excused himself.

When he went out of the courtroom, Alan was able to look down from the balcony on the third floor which also served as an alley. Below, in front of the building, he saw a taxi parked with its doors open. *There they were!* Tina and Dennis, the latter holding Baby Al, entered the backseat. Tanya shared the front seat with the driver.

"Tina!"

But Alan's loud voice was unheard as the doors of the taxi were shut, and it pulled away quickly from the vicinity of the metropolitan court. Sinking in frustration, Alan still managed to conduct inquiries and found that, indeed, Tina and Dennis were married in one of the court branches in the building.

***

The apprentice mate was slow-paced and moved as though he was reluctant to proceed and uncertain as to whether he should continue with his planned pursuit or simply withdraw and pull back from the area which was the frontage of Tina's residence, the same place where he had knocked the day before and received the bad news from the person behind the door.

After a painstaking evaluation of the course of action he had to take, Alan chose to pursue with his planned visit. He decided to knock on the door and this time, when it opened, it was Dennis who appeared before him.

Alan, prompted by impulse, grabbed the collar of Dennis' shirt and blurted out: "I'm a classmate and a friend of yours, Dennis, why did you have to do this? You know Tina and I have an issue and we're supposed to marry each other. Why did you take the opportunity…?"

"I'm sorry, Alan, we were convinced you're dead. We never expected you'd come back alive…."

Suddenly, Tina and Tanya showed up, the former coming from the kitchen while the latter descending from the upper floor of the house. Karen was holding Baby Al, following Tanya. Tina immediately interceded for Dennis, shielding him from Alan who was being pulled back and held by Tanya.

"I'm sorry, Alan …." And Tina re-echoed the line of justification raised by Dennis. "Don't take it against us, Alan. We will not deprive you of your right over Baby Al."

Alan pretended he did not hear Tina as he turned his attention to his son, taking him away from Karen and cuddling him, manifesting the intensity of his emotion as he let the baby boy cling to him.

As Alan focused his attention to his son, Tina and Dennis whispered to each other and were quick on letting out a proposal. "You can have weekends with Baby Al."

"Yes, Alan," Tanya interrupted. "I undertake to handle the conveyance of your son on weekends. You aren't going to miss him. It's a mission I impose upon myself. It's some kind of well-being that is involved here, a sort of atonement on our part."

"Thanks for your concern, Tanya." It was all that Alan could utter. He had condescended and made known to all of them his desire to be with Baby Al on the last Sunday of August.

Part 5:
As Fate Would Have It

Chapter Twenty-one

The last Sunday of August, 1990, fell on the twenty-sixth day of the month and it was a time for people in Manila to commemorate and celebrate the deeds of their heroes, inspiring the later generations to cherish and protect the freedom gained through the martyrdom of their ancestors. Tanya and Alan took Baby Al to a mall and witnessed the memorabilia put up by the management to induce the shoppers into an appreciation of the bequest from heroes and martyrs.

Later in the afternoon, they entered a restaurant in the mall and had refreshment there. Tanya took out a feeding bottle from her shoulder bag and let Baby Al enjoy the nourishment as they waited for their own.

"I'm sorry, Alan, it was never the intention of Tina and Dennis to hurt you. They really were of the belief that you're gone and wouldn't be seen again," Tanya unexpectedly expressed her remorse to Alan.

"It's all right, Tanya, I've come to full realization that perhaps no one deserves the blame but myself for all that had come up," Alan assuaged the heavy emotion that was about to overwhelm Tanya.

"Thanks, Alan, for understanding our plight and bearing with us for our inadequacies."

"Don't mention it, Tanya. The healing process has begun."

The subsequent Sunday was the first for the month of September, 1990, falling on the second day of the month, and it was a finer day than the previous. Tanya and Alan brought Baby Al to the church as they started their day out early.

After the mass, they went to a park and roamed about until they found that noon was nearing. They went to a mall for lunch and whiled away the afternoon until the sun inched closer to the horizon.

Before they called it a day, Alan came up with a suggestion to Tanya. "Suppose we spend it in a beach next Sunday?"

"Why not, indeed? A nice idea," Tanya agreed.

The next Sunday was the ninth day of the month. And to prepare for the things they would be needing in the beach, Alan and Tanya met on the Saturday afternoon, attended an anticipated mass in a chapel and thereafter went shopping for the provisions intended for the following day.

They set out for the beach early in the morning of the ninth of September. When they arrived there, Alan chose a cottage with a single room where Baby Al would be comfortable while sleeping.

"The weather seems to cooperate with us," Tanya commented.

"And the water is clear," Alan observed.

They had lunch in the cottage after having submerged themselves in the water with Baby Al at a shallow portion of the beach. In a little while, the baby was asleep.

"It's still hot out there. We might as well relax here with Baby Al in the cottage," Tanya suggested while adjusting the fitness of her bathing suit. "Sorry if I look awkward in this suit."

"You look gorgeous in it, Tanya."

"You're magnificent in your swimming trunk, too, Alan."

Silence prevailed for a few minutes. It was Alan who broke it.

"Learning what happened to you was too painful for me, Tanya," Alan said.

Tanya was disconcerted as she did not expect it from Alan. She managed to respond calmly, though. "I'm trying to get it over with, Alan. I'll get by."

"I'll help you run off it, Tanya."

Tanya was beginning to experience a strange feeling. She was able to utter some words, nevertheless. "I'll return the favor, Alan. Let me help you too extricate yourself from the dilemma created by Tina and Dennis."

"No necessity for it, Tanya."

"What do you mean?"

"Did you notice how quickly I managed to return to my composed self despite the searing effect of what Tina and Dennis had done?"

"Why, Alan?"

"Because I could no longer deny it—and neither could I continue playing blind to the fact that it's you who move my life, Tanya, not Tina."

"Alan? I don't understand ..."

"You're the real love of my life, Tanya."

Tanya was at a loss for words, grasping at anything she could utter. "Did your visit to me at the hotel in Kuwait, Alan, have something to do with it?"

"Precisely. I did, not because you're Tina's sister but because you're *you.*"

"Stop it, Alan. I can't bear ..." And Tanya began to cry.

"You have to know it, Tanya, as my own self tells me now it's the real score."

"But ..."

"I went for Tina because I thought in the past you were beyond my reach. I had the impression that you were bound for the convent. My feeling then was that, Tina was your perfect personification."

"Alan, please ..."

"But I've come into full realization now, Tanya. You could never be duplicated. There's no way you could ever be cloned. While you were perfect for the nunnery, Tina was a bit flirty ... Pardon me for the comment, Tanya. It's the truth, however."

"She's still my sister, Alan."

"And she's still the mother of my son."

Once again, silence prevailed for a while.

"Tanya, let's put everything behind us. Why don't we start building life once more with each other?" Alan pleaded with Tanya.

"I'm not anymore in a position to do that, Alan. I've been ruined," Tanya sobbed.

"No, Tanya, you've only been initiated into the realities of life," Alan was likewise teary-eyed as he stressed his point.

"Alan, I don't think I'm prepared for anything ..."

Tanya was not able to finish her words as Alan held her shoulders and drew her closer to him. She was not able to resist Alan's clasp. Then she felt Alan's lips touching her own.

"No, Alan," Tanya became defensive.

Alan, however, did not relent. His lips moved down to Tanya's neck, to her nape and further down to pursue an encircling route while easing out the bathing suit from her body. Tanya writhed, as if in pain.

"Tanya, don't think of anything. Don't recall the past. Put this in your mind—that in this world, there's only you and me ... now!"

"Alan, it's too difficult to place anything in my mind. It's all pain that I feel ..."

"Tanya, think of me ... think of your deliverance!" Alan stressed as he slid down fully Tanya's bathing suit and doing away with his own swimming trunk too.

"I can't, Alan, they're getting back into my consciousness!"

"Who are they?"

"The soldiers—the sergeant leading them."

"Cast them out of your mind, Tanya. They're gone. They no longer exist."

"The pain that was created subsists, Alan."

"Close your eyes, Tanya, and don't fantasize. Think only of me and you!"

Alan guided Tanya in lying down beside Baby Al who was in deep sleep but there was still resistance on her part as her feet moved, kicking away accidentally her bathing suit and Alan's swimming trunk to the floor. But the more she struggled, the stranger things turned into as she ultimately likened herself to a candle liquefying.

As Alan pushed himself deeper into Tanya's consciousness, the latter wriggled and almost passed out, but a different kind of agitation struck her and she suddenly awakened into ecstasy, something that she never felt before, something different from what intruded into her during that fateful night at the *QRH*. She tussled, making a way out for herself from something which had a binding effect, and when she stretched her hands to get hold of anything within her reach, she quivered. She moaned and heaved a breath, lifting her spirits—until her legs trembled and shifted, touching the feeding bottle beside Baby Al. It rolled down to the floor and the milk it retained spilled until it was drained of its content.

"You kicked and emptied Baby Al's bottle," Alan told Tanya when it was over. "The baby's awake now."

"Don't panic, Alan, we'll find a way …" Tanya held Baby Al in her arms and pressed the baby upon her bosom. "Just to entertain Al."

"Like you entertained me."

Tanya pinched Alan in his right arm.

"Let's hurry back home and turn over Baby Al to Tina. She has got bigger feeding tools than what you have with you."

Tanya pinched Alan again, this time in his waist.

"Oh, Tanya, I'd always cherish those pinches from you," he said as he started to wear his clothes again.

***

On that day in another island—a different Asian country—there was a gloomy atmosphere. Nothing in the sky was foreboding of rain but of the haze which had the tendency to intensify. If it did, that would be characteristic of the murk which dwelt in the hearts of men hiding in a portion of the island's central forest, four of whom were now seen trudging along a rugged terrain. The path they were taking led to a river which, when crossed, would end up in clustered huts behind a tree-lined secret village.

When the men arrived in front of the biggest of the huts, a bearded man not less than fifty years of age came down to meet them.

One of the four men introduced to him another man beside him. "He's here—our new recruit."

"I am delighted to see you. Thank you for believing in our cause," the bearded man declared, addressing the new recruit.

"I'm delighted, too, supreme leader. It is a distinct honor to be of service to the cause," the new recruit responded.

After a brief ritualistic encounter, the supreme leader said, "Welcome to the Cougar Unit of the Tamil Liberation Movement, Comrade Derik."

"Thank you, comrade," Derik said.

Epilogue

Epilogue: And Hope, too...

On August 2, 1991, the first anniversary of the Iraqi incursion into Kuwait was celebrated in the Philippines by the management of *Stripes Shipping Corporation* with three of their Japanese principals as guests of honor. It was actually a celebration not meant to give significance to the invasion but such date happened to be the ETD, or at least the eve thereof, of one of their ships, *M/V Hope*, which disappeared under mysterious circumstances in the Persian Gulf, the last known exact location of which was the port of Kuwait.

The venue of the affair was a big hotel in downtown Manila and it kicked off at nine o'clock in the morning, as it was not intended to be a purely an activity for those present to dine and wine but to witness a mass wedding.

When the program began, the local manager of the shipping company hosted the ceremonies.

"The management of this company, with full support from our principals based in Tokyo, Japan, would like to extend to all of you our profound gratitude for the full support you have given us, especially in trying times. Before we go full swing with the occasion, let us bow our heads and offer a minute of silence for all those who have perished while discharging their functions and duties in Kuwait in the height of the storm a year ago."

The silence lasted longer than a minute.

"We in the management are delighted to afford our beneficiaries a chance to wed their loved ones in a religious rite. Let us now welcome them and the officiating priest as we start with the mass."

The mass was conducted in an hour and a half. As his concluding message, the celebrant said—"For all the inequities and sins that we may have committed, there's always forgiveness that waits; and when it is invoked, its outpouring will be profuse. Let us join those who are forthright in their remorse, for their contrition is the key towards unraveling a new life we shall look forward to."

When it was over, the program's host took back the microphone.

"A significant announcement will be relayed to you by our company's chairman of the board. Sir ... please ..." And the local manager turned over the microphone to his boss.

The speaker did not make his announcement perfunctory. He attached to it the significance bruited about.

"It was sad to lose hope, but everything did not end there. We can regain it, as we do now. Although *M/V Hope* is no longer with us, *M/V Hope 2* is sailing soon."

A stirred excitement permeated the function area as the board chairman continued with his speech.

"Captain Eldon Ramos will be the master of the new ship."

Loud clapping of hands immediately reverberated through the hall.

"He will be ably assisted by his chief officer, Peter Singh, who is one of our newly wed couples, with his lovely wife—now Myra Singh. Congratulations and best wishes, Chief Mate and Mrs. Singh!"

An even louder clapping of hands ensued.

"Second Mate Ben Gomez will be on board also."

The clapping of hands continued.

"Third Mate Alan Blancaflor will be on board as well. Congratulations, Alan, on being a licensed third mate now and for taking a lovely bride. Our newly wed third officer is with his wife Tanya—now Mrs. Blancaflor. Best wishes!"

It was the loudest clapping of hands. The hall was in uproar.

"Of course, we've guests who joined our mass wedding. Congratulations and best wishes to Dennis Nillos and wife Tina. By the way, Dennis is coming back to his profession. He will be joining *M/V Hope 2* as an apprentice mate. In less than a year's time, being half-way with the experience, he will be third mate also."

The unexpected announcement gave rise to a resounding applause.

"And for our special guests, we have a couple from France. Welcome former Corporal Charles Ubaud of the Kuwaiti police and wife Grace, our very own, who had always dreamed of a church wedding here in the Philippines."

The applause continued as the audience waited for the last words from the speaker.

"*M/V Hope 2* is a different kind of ship. Unlike the first which was a cargo vessel, the second is a cruise ship and will be plying the southeastern route in Asia."

The audience reacted excitedly with a—"Wow!"

And the speaker concluded his speech: "Major cities in the region will be our destination—except one. We have deleted from our itinerary the port city of Ceylon—what is now known as Sri Lanka."

As they gathered to take their lunch, the newlyweds talked about the future in store for them.

"Alan, I hope you'll pass on to me everything you've known for an apprentice mate to become a successful third mate," Dennis said to Alan.

"Of course," Alan assured.

"Give the proper guidance to Dennis, please, Alan," Tina requested. "He has long been out of the ship."

"Don't worry, sister, Alan will do it. He's the only guy who had been given an assignment as third mate—of both *M/V Hope* 1 and 2," Tanya smiled and commented. "He's also one guy who's lucky enough to serve the best of both worlds."

Tina squinted at her sister but the latter simply took it in stride and held on to her smile.

And they all chuckled as the other newlyweds came nearer to join them in the conversation.

###

AUTHOR'S NOTE

This book is a work of fiction and is actually a presentation of various realities in life which the overseas contract workers have to face as they pursue a belief that financial healing lies somewhere. This is likewise a revelation of the nostalgia and dilemma that they have to contend with in leaving their land of birth for such pursuit. The characters created herein are purely fictional and any similarity or resemblance to actual persons is purely coincidental. The places described, however, are real and the events that transpire forming as backdrop of the story may have actually happened. Inclusion of aspects thereof is imperative to give flavor to the story.

The author is motivated solely by a desire to provide entertainment to the readers, and no offense, if any, is intended to an individual or group, be it as to their beliefs or well-being.

ACKNOWLEDGMENT

The author acknowledges the invaluable help and assistance he obtained from various sectors in the preparation of this book and his other works previously published as well as those still being prepared for publication.

His appreciation goes to those who shared with him their full support and positive stance as well as their kind indulgence as the author gropes along the pathways to self-publication.

Such regard likewise extends to the members of his family, peers and friends who in one way or another have taken part in making this venture a success.

The author is furthermore indebted to his readers for their patronage of his works and staying with him in the journey through pages of the printed word.

ABOUT THE AUTHOR

The author, 62 years of age, now resides in Iloilo City, Philippines, where he is a member of the *Sumakwelan*, an organization of vernacular writers from the Western Visayan region and portions of Mindanao Island in the Philippines.

His works include several titles in non-fiction and some in fiction and poetry. He has been engaged in vernacular writing in his country since he was a teen-ager. He is currently working on the translation of his literary works into the English language. He assures his readers, however, of his earnest efforts in seeing to it that nothing is missed in the course of the translation.

The author may be reached at this e-mail address—nrcsbookshop@ymail.com.

His availability may be had also through:
*www.twitter.com/narmabooks
*www.scribd.com/narmabooks

He may be visited at the following Web sites:
*http://narmabooks.webs.com
*http://narmabooks2.wordpress.com

Narma Books

We are on Facebook. See us—

Click on **www.facebook.com** and search for:
Narma Books

We are on Twitter, too.

Follow us—
www.twitter.com/narmabooks

View us on Pinterest—
www.pinterest.com/narmabooks

Find us on Scribd—
www.scribd.com/narmabooks

Read our inspirational shares and selections:
Click on—

http://nrcsinspirational.wordpress.com

Other works

Other works of fiction from Narma Books dealing with Mideast are the following:

The Fall of Damascus—The Middle East is the focus of the incidents in this novel. The drama unfolding as the episodes progress highlights the events in Syria, although the author has emphasized that this is not a war story; rather, it is some kind of a love story taking the reader into an extended tour of various places, particularly Europe. The main characters though are of Asian descent.

This book is available in print version:
www.createspace.com/4734005
Or in e-book version:
www.amazon.com/dp/B00J94FXPK

The novel is likewise available as an e-book via **www.smashwords.com**.

Harvest of Sand—tells us of a turmoil in the Middle East and how foreign lives were affected. It is an account of events which transpired in the Middle East in 1990 spawned by Iraq's incursion into Kuwait. On August 2, 1990 in Kuwait City, it was getting late but Brian Rios, a deputy employment and welfare attaché assigned at the Philippine Embassy there, knew he was facing a sleepless night. More people would be arriving and would be joining the multitude of those who were already jostled in the embassy premises. The succeeding scenes were unnerving.

The story is included in the author's collection of his other works of fiction, *"Fiction Assemblage,"* made up of a novella and four short stories which are available either in print or in e-book format.

The collection may be procured online through— *https://www.createspace.com/3598890.*

More Books from the Author:

Fiction

* **A Man and A Girl**

    - Available as one of the collected stories in Fiction Assemblage

* **An Awakening and Losing**

    - Available at: **www.createspace.com/3565490**

* **Menace on the Face of the Red Moon**

    - Available at: **www.createspace.com/3571177**

Non-fiction

o **Proof, Admissions and Presumptions**

    - Available at: **www.createspace.com/3542950**

o **Things You Encounter on the Way to Court**

    - Available at: **www.createspace.com/3560703**

o **Crime, Retribution and Exoneration**

- Available at: **www.createspace.com/3697327**

Inspirational:

-- Finding Pathways through the Community
- Available in print and as an e-book:
www.createspace.com/3747127

-o0o-